T0329208

# A killer confidante?

"Your father sounds like a wise man," Diva said.

Jo nodded. "He was."

"He passed away?" Diva asked.

"Yes. He . . ." He was murdered. All because the justice system he loved had been corrupted by the drug trade.

"You don't have to tell me about it," Diva said softly. "I know how difficult it is to talk about these things."

In the reflection of the mirror over the vanity table, Jo saw Diva's face grow dark. "You obviously have your own tragedies to deal with," she said.

Diva sighed. "My hair used to be beautiful—it was a shiny, midnight black."

"It's still beautiful." Jo decided against pressing further. If Diva wanted to talk, she would.

"This . . ." She pointed to the stripe in her hair. "It hasn't always been there."

"No?" Now Jo's curiosity was uncontainable. "How did it get that way?"

"Part of my hair turned white the day my father—" Her voice broke, and she began to sob.

Don't miss any books in this thrilling new series:

*#1 License to Thrill*
*#2 Live and Let Spy*
*#3 Nobody Does It Better*
*#4 Spy Girls Are Forever*
*#5 Dial "V" for Vengeance*
*#6 If Looks Could Kill ⋆*

Available from ARCHWAY Paperbacks

⋆ Coming soon

# Dial "V" for Vengeance

## by
## Elizabeth Cage

**AN ARCHWAY PAPERBACK**
Published by POCKET BOOKS
New York   London   Toronto   Sydney   Tokyo   Singapore

AN ARCHWAY PAPERBACK *Original*

An Archway Paperback published by
POCKET BOOKS, a division of Simon & Schuster Inc.
1230 Avenue of the Americas, New York, NY 10020

Spy Girls™ is a trademark of 17th Street Productions,
a division of Daniel Weiss Associates, Inc.

Produced by 17th Street Productions,
a division of Daniel Weiss Associates, Inc.
33 West 17th Street, New York, NY 10011

ISBN: 978-1-4814-2084-6

First Archway Paperback printing May 1999

10  9  8  7  6  5  4  3  2  1

AN ARCHWAY PAPERBACK and colophon are registered trademarks of Simon & Schuster Inc.

Printed in the U.S.A.

IL 7+

*For Gage and Wendy—congratulations!*

# Dial "V" for Vengeance

**M**aybe Uncle Sam is finally going to reveal his true identity to us," Jo Carreras suggested to her fellow Spy Girls as the trio walked down the long hallway leading to their boss's office. "We've never been summoned directly to his personal headquarters."

Jo was endlessly awed by the rooms and corridors that constituted The Tower. Unlike most government agencies, The Tower was all about future shock—clean lines and smooth surfaces. There were massive, sectional leather sofas all over the place, and a seriously impressive collection of modern art lined the walls. Kind of like something she pictured when she read the book *1984*, but without all that nasty totalitarianism stuff. Jo couldn't wait to get inside Uncle Sam's office—no doubt, the place would be totally decked out.

"Yeah, right." Theresa Hearth snorted, responding to Jo. "You *know* why the great one has summoned us."

Okay, so there was no way in you-know-what that Uncle Sam was going to let them see his face. A girl could dream.

"Get ready, *chicas*," Caylin Pike announced, flipping her blond hair over one shoulder. "We're about to learn all about mission number five."

Caylin and Theresa were right, of course. The dynamic trio had been back at Tower headquarters in D.C. for almost two days. Their Swiss mission had been successfully completed, and now it was time for a new assignment.

Jo felt a flutter of excitement as the girls neared Uncle Sam's office. Nothing got the old adrenaline flowing like the prospect of yet another top secret mission. She picked up her pace, impatient to reach Uncle Sam's lair.

And there was no doubt that her fellow Spy Girls were equally anxious to find out the itinerary of the next adventure. Over the past few months Jo had more or less mastered the ability to read Caylin and Theresa's minds. It was hard to believe that less than a year ago, the three young women had been strangers.

Jo would never forget the morning she had arrived at The Tower for the first time. She had thought she was about to matriculate in an elite East Coast college. Uh, try not! Long story short, it turned out that Jo (the linguist)—

along with Caylin (the athlete) and Theresa (the computer nerd)—had been carefully selected by the U.S. government to be trained as a top secret super-duper spy team. After some of the most intense training Jo could have imagined, the girls were officially inducted into The Tower. Voilà! The Spy Girls were born, and the ride of a lifetime had begun.

"Ready or not, here we come," Jo called out as she pushed on Uncle Sam's heavy metal door.

Yep. The office was ultraspiffy. Huge glass desk, a Rothko hanging next to a floor-to-ceiling window, and several long leather couches.

"Greetings, Spy Girls." Uncle Sam's gravelly voice—gravelly-sexy, not gravelly-gross—was loud and clear, but as per usual, The Man himself was nowhere to be seen. Instead a digitally programmed, ultrapixelated version of Uncle Sam's silhouette appeared before the trio on a large screen. "You're all looking extremely well."

Jo plopped onto a black leather sofa. "So, where are we going next?" she asked. "Dallas, Texas? Zimbabwe, Africa? Sydney, Australia?"

"We'd like to go somewhere warm," Theresa said. "I've been hoping for a chance to try out one of those solar-powered laptops."

"And headquarters complete with an Olympic-sized pool wouldn't be too shabby," Caylin added.

Uncle Sam laughed. "You're going to Brazil."

"Brazil, as in home of the samba and incredibly good-looking Latin lovers Brazil?" Caylin asked.

"That's the one," Uncle Sam confirmed. "But go easy on the good-looking Latin lovers. You all will be there to work."

"So, what are we going to be doing in South America?" Jo asked. "Besides working on our tans, of course."

Uncle Sam cleared his throat—a sure sign that he was about to impart a piece of crucial, possibly terrifying, information. "The Tower has received an anonymous tip from an informant in Rio," he said solemnly. "We have every reason to believe that this informant has influence within Rio de Janeiro's thriving underworld."

"And what does said informant claim is going down?" Theresa asked. "Tell us exactly what we're dealing with."

As usual, Theresa was the Spy Girl most concerned with getting facts, details, and an outlined plan of action. In Jo's experience, attention to minutiae was a trait common to most computer geekettes.

## Dial "V" for Vengeance

"The informant promises to lead us to the head of one of Brazil's largest drug-smuggling rings," Uncle Sam stated. "If you girls complete this mission successfully, some of the most dangerous people in South America will be rendered powerless."

"Wow . . . big-time stuff," Caylin murmured.

"That's right," Uncle Sam agreed. "This drug lord has the blood of hundreds—if not thousands—of people on his hands."

Jo felt as if a small, homemade bomb had just exploded in her stomach. Drugs. Drug lords. Drug cartels. The words had a powerful effect on her. All visions of bikinis and cute guys faded from her mind. In their place was the face of her father. Four years ago Jo's beloved dad, a highly respected Miami judge, had been murdered—all because he had been presiding over a case involving a powerful drug lord. Since then, nothing had been the same. . . .

"This so-called tip sounds a little thin," Caylin said. "I mean, does this informant have a name?"

"Maybe someone is setting a trap," Theresa agreed. "This whole thing sounds too good to be true. Fly to Rio. Meet informant. Bring down major drug lord, all as easy as one-two-three."

"Good point, Theresa," Uncle Sam said. "It's

always possible that informants have ulterior motives." He paused. "I'm counting on you three to discern whether or not the informant's motives are trustworthy."

"We won't let you down, Sam," Jo promised. To heck with the informant. She would track down the underworld baddie herself if necessary. "We'll bring these people down . . . no matter what the cost."

"So much for the concept of R and R," Caylin muttered an hour later. "I'm beginning to wonder why we ever bother to unpack."

The trio had gone straight from Uncle Sam's office to their Tower dorm room, the floor of which was now covered with clothes.

"I still have shinsplints from skiing in Switzerland," Theresa said, picking up a pair of mud-splattered jeans. "Jeez, where have these *been?*"

Caylin tossed aside a limp, tattered bikini. "Let's hope we each get a complete new wardrobe at the Rio headquarters. I have nothing decent to wear."

"How about you, Jo?" Theresa asked. "Are your duds in the same sorry shape as ours?"

"Yeah, no—I mean, sorry, what did you say?" Jo sounded dazed, as if she had heard nothing of Theresa and Caylin's fifteen-minute discourse on the nonlucky series of events that had led to their too quick departure from The Tower.

Caylin tossed a pair of fraying cotton panties into the trash can and glanced at Jo. She was sitting on her bed, staring at the still empty suitcase in front of her.

"Are you all right, Jo?" Caylin asked. "'Cause we're, like, under some major time pressure here."

"This is going to be our most dangerous mission yet," Jo predicted darkly. "Drug lords don't mess around."

"Why doesn't Sam have something more solid for us to go on?" Caylin asked, struggling unsuccessfully to keep the whine out of her tone. "I mean, we're just supposed to jet to Rio and meet some random informant in a night-club called El Centro."

"That's not a lot of information to go on," Jo agreed. "But it will have to do."

Theresa slipped her laptop computer into its carry-on bag. "All we know is that we're supposed to look for a red flower and gray-streaked hair." She paused. "Is the old guy going to be holding a rose between his teeth or what?"

"Look on the bright side," Caylin said. "If the informant is going gray, we're pretty much guaranteed that we won't be distracted by any pesky romantic notions."

"Nobody said being a Spy Girl was going to be all fun and games," Jo said sharply. "Let's remember what we're going to South America to accomplish."

"Easy, Carreras," Theresa admonished. "Caylin and I take our missions just as seriously as you do."

Then something clicked in Caylin's head. Man, she was an idiot. And so was Theresa. How could they have been so insensitive? Going to Brazil to fight a drug lord wasn't going to be just another mission for Jo. In many ways, she would be evening a score.

Caylin shot Theresa a warning glance. They both needed to let Jo know but pronto that they would be behind her every step of the way as she confronted the demons of her past. Yes. It was definitely time for an official Spy Girl powwow. Unless they all addressed what Jo was going through, their fellow James Bondette might not make it through this mission with her sanity.

Jo stared into space, reliving in vivid Technicolor the day of her father's murder. She closed her eyes against the painful memory, but the images wouldn't go away. For probably the thousandth time since Judge Carreras died her freshman year in high school, Jo found her mind replaying each tragic detail.

*"Be good today, Josefina," Mr. Carreras commanded. "I don't want to hear from Ms. Pinsky that you got sent to the principal's office again."*

*They were sitting in the front seat of Mr. Carreras's aging car in front of Josefina's Miami high school. As he did every morning, Mr. Carreras was dropping off Jo on his way to the courthouse, where he would spend the day listening to prosecutors and defense lawyers pleading their cases before a court of law. Josefina had expected her dad to be in an awesome mood today—he had just finished a high-profile drug case that had consumed his every waking moment for six months.*

*And he was in a good mood. Unfortunately, on this particular morning Josefina's father also seemed determined to give her a lecture on the virtues of being an obedient member of the student body.*

*Josefina sighed. "Dad, I'm not going to apologize for getting into trouble last week. I don't believe in cruelty to animals, and I absolutely refuse to dissect a poor, defenseless frog."*

*Mr. Carreras raised one bushy eyebrow. "Even if that means you will fail biology, Josefina?"*

9

She nodded vigorously. "I will not back down on this issue, Dad. It's too important."

Mr. Carreras laughed, then reached over and patted Josefina on the head. "My daughter, the crusader." For a moment he stared into her eyes. "I want you to do well in school . . . but I also believe in standing up for what you believe in." Again he paused. "Someday you're going to make a difference in this world, Josefina."

She grinned. She knew her father would come around eventually. He had devoted too much of his life to doing good to undermine his only daughter's efforts—however humble—to change the world.

"Thanks, Daddy." Josefina leaned forward to hug her father before she left the car. Then suddenly, the peace of her morning was shattered.

Pop. Pop.

She whirled around and screamed.

A man had placed a gun to her father's head and pulled the trigger. Two terrible shots that changed Josefina's life forever. As she rushed to her dying father's side, his last words echoed through her mind. Someday she would make a difference. Someday.

"Jo? Are you okay?" Theresa's soft voice broke through Jo's tortured memories, and her eyes fluttered open.

"Yeah, I was just . . . remembering." She was surprised to see that tears were falling onto the legs of her jeans. Jo hadn't even realized that she was crying.

"We know this is going to be tough for you," Caylin said.

Jo dried the tears from her cheeks as sadness was replaced with anger. "I still can't believe that the man who shot my father never went to jail."

Theresa shook her head in sympathy. "I don't understand how the defense claimed there was a lack of evidence. Somebody must have paid off an official."

Jo shrugged. "Who knows?" She tried not to dwell on the details of the investigation surrounding her father's murder. In fact, she had blocked out most of the time immediately following that horrible morning. She simply couldn't deal with the injustice that had allowed her father's killer to go free.

"But the police were positive that your father's murder was connected to the trial of a drug lord," Theresa said. "Which probably means this mission is going to be extra hard on you."

Jo nodded. She knew firsthand how ruthless the drug trade was. The people who got rich selling white powder didn't care how many lives they destroyed. As long as they had their fancy cars and mansions, they were happy.

"I just have a bad feeling about going to Rio," Jo admitted to her friends. "We've been in over our heads before . . . but this is different."

"Theresa and I won't leave your side for a moment," Caylin said reassuringly. "Besides, we may fly to Brazil and discover that the informant's information is no good."

Theresa nodded. "Yeah, we could be on a plane heading back to The Tower two days from now."

"I have to confess that there's a part of me that hopes this trip *doesn't* pan out," Jo said softly. "As much as I despise everything having anything to do with drugs, I also have a feeling that this whole mission is going to be an emotional roller coaster."

"That's not the Jo I know," Caylin answered. "You're usually the first one of us who's ready to risk anything to fight the bad guys."

Caylin was right. Jo remembered the steely resolve she had felt in Uncle Sam's office. This was an important mission. Jo couldn't allow her personal history to get in the way.

"We'll be with you every step of the way," Theresa reminded her. "The three of us will get through this mission together."

Jo smiled. Bonding with Theresa and Caylin had been the best part of her new life as a spy for

The Tower. They filled a place in her life that had been emptied when her father was killed. They made her feel safe and secure—no matter how dire any given situation seemed on the surface.

"You guys are right on," Jo said. "If it turns out that the gray-haired guy is for real, then I'll fight with everything I've got to put this drug lord where he belongs—in memory of my dad."

"He would have been so proud of you, Jo." Theresa plopped down next to Jo and threw an arm around her shoulders. "I'm sure he'll be watching over us while we're in Brazil."

Jo took a deep, calming breath. From this moment forward, she was going to put her all into this mission. For her father. For justice.

"Enough gloom and doom," Jo announced suddenly, bouncing up from the bed. "Life is for the living!"

Caylin shoved her suitcase into the corner. "You said it, Spy Girl. Let's do something fun—preferably an activity that doesn't involve packing."

Jo walked to her CD collection and pulled out one of her all-time favorite discs. "All right, *chiquitas.* It's time you learned how to samba!"

Theresa stood up, kicking aside a pile of clothes to make room. "Me, dancing?" She laughed. "Now *this* is going to be dangerous!"

think I'm going to like this mission more than I expected," Jo commented the next afternoon. "The guys in Rio simply define the word *hot*."

Theresa surveyed the crowded airport over the rims of her large black sunglasses—part of the glam-girl disguise she had been assigned back at The Tower. "I don't like to encourage obsession over testosterone, but you're right."

Caylin pulled a tube of lipstick out of her leopard-print handbag. "Anyone else care for a touch-up? You never know when Mr. Wonderful is going to appear."

"There will be plenty of time to give each other makeovers later," Theresa said. "Right now, let's concentrate on finding our headquarters."

"I know *Theresa* is uptight, but does 'Trixie' ever let her hair down?" Jo asked, wiggling her eyebrows underneath the wide brim of an orange straw hat.

Theresa groaned. She wasn't thrilled with

15

her latest alias. Who was going to take a girl named Trixie seriously? "Listen, *Jacinta,* I'm still Theresa underneath this thousand-dollar outfit."

"Personally, I *like* being Corinne, wealthy New York debutante," Caylin chirped. "It's a trip. And yet not too far from the truth."

"Ha ha." Theresa adjusted the rhinestone-studded collar of her jacket. During the past few months she had gotten used to doing the changing-skins thang. The Tower insisted the three Spy Girls use different disguises for each mission—still, she missed her old khakis and T-shirts. "Can't I be a poor, badly dressed deb?" Theresa lamented.

Caylin shook her head. "Poor debutantes aren't interested in pouring tens of thousands of dollars into drugs to take back to the United States."

"Oh. Right." Faking an interest in "getting into the business" was going to be tough, but she had to do what she had to do. "So, are we going to figure out where we're going, or are we going to stand around here and talk fashion all day?"

Jo glanced at the electronic organizer that held the girls' immediate instructions. "Our wheels should be right outside this door." She pointed left.

16

## Dial "V" for Vengeance

The girls walked out of the airport and into the fading Brazilian sunlight. The air was warm and moist, tropical. Theresa had heard about Rio's famous Carnival season, and she could see that this was the perfect place for extended celebration. People streamed across the airport sidewalks dressed in bright clothes, laughing and greeting one another with hugs and kisses.

"Hello, babe mobile!" Jo shouted. "I think *that* pretty little thing is our ride for the next few days."

"Nice!" Caylin yelled, running toward the black Alfa Romeo that Jo had discovered. "I think I'm *really* going to like being a wealthy New York debutante."

"Give me a black Alfa Romeo and a fabulous new wardrobe, and I'll curtsy for as many stuffed shirts as you want me to," Jo agreed. She slid the key she had been handed at their final Tower briefing into the driver's-side door of the Alfa Romeo. "Score. It's ours."

Theresa placed her laptop in the tiny backseat of the Alfa Romeo and climbed inside. "It's a good thing Uncle Sam called our room and said we didn't need to worry about packing much. I don't think we could fit more than one small garment bag in this thing."

Caylin got into the car and slammed the

door shut. "I've never really pictured myself as a Euro-flash kind of chick before, but I think I could get used to this."

"Do we have the address?" Theresa asked.

Jo pushed a red flashing button on the dashboard of the Alfa Romeo. Instantly an electronic map of Rio appeared on a miniature screen. "Check."

"Then let's hit it," Caylin said. "If this is our car, I can't wait to get a look at our pad."

Jo twisted her black hair up into a topknot and revved the engine. "Home, James!" She put the Alfa Romeo in gear and peeled out of the Rio airport with her usual dramatic flair.

For the next half hour Theresa relaxed against the Alfa Romeo's black leather seats as Jo navigated the car through the streets of Rio. Despite her semi–nervous breakdown the night before, Jo seemed to have rallied. Thank goodness for that. Since Jo was the only one of the three teens who could speak Portuguese, it was imperative that she be in top form. Not that Theresa had entertained doubts about Jo's ability to rise to the occasion. The girl had guts coming out of her nose.

"Okay, girls," Jo announced finally, slamming on the brakes of the Alfa Romeo. "Four-fourteen Hacienda Drive. Home sweet home."

Theresa opened her eyes and looked out the

window. "I thought we were staying at a house! This place is a hotel."

Caylin laughed. "Wrong, my friend. *This* is the kind of place three footloose and oh-so-fancy-free debs rent for a stint in South America."

Theresa whistled softly. The house wasn't a house. It was a bona fide mansion. And it was pink. In front of the place was a huge circular drive and a large fountain. "I feel like Cinderella at the big ball. What happens at midnight?"

Jo switched off the engine. "*Vámonos,* Spy Girls. Our mansion awaits."

"We can look at our new clothes and practice acting vapid," Caylin said as she opened the passenger-side door. "Like, hi, I'm, like, Corinne, and I, like, love to shop and go sailing on my million-dollar yacht."

"Hey, this is going to be a piece of cake," Jo said. "All we have to do is leave our brains in the walk-in closet."

Theresa climbed out of the Alfa Romeo and followed her friends toward the ten-foot-high front doors. Whether their personas were vapid or not, this was going to be one mission to put in the record book.

"Rio, here we come," she murmured. "Ready or not."

\*    \*    \*

Remember the mission. Remember the mission. Jo repeated the mantra to herself again and again as she applied yet one more layer of black mascara to her long eyelashes. She was in a white marble bathroom, wearing a five-thousand-dollar beaded designer dress. A week ago those two facts would have added up to heaven on earth in her mind.

But Jo couldn't shake the foreboding that had descended upon her as she, Caylin, and Theresa had explored their decked-out deb den. Yes, their over-the-top house had been outfitted by The Tower in order to provide them with an airtight cover story. But Jo knew that there were many other mansions in Rio that were even more elaborately decorated. And each piece of avant-garde furniture had been paid for in cash—cash earned from selling drugs. The notion made her nauseous.

A tap on the door interrupted Jo's gloomy interior monologue. "Hey, *Jacinta*, can we invade your private space?" Caylin called.

Jo set down her mascara wand and pasted a fake smile on her face. "Yeah, *entre.*"

The door opened, and Theresa tottered into the bathroom, wearing a pair of five-inch stiletto heels. "I don't know how much help I'm going to be tracking down our mystery informant if I trip and break my ankle on these things," she moaned. "Don't debs ever wear, like, high-tops?"

Caylin perched on the edge of the sunken marble bathtub and regarded her own rhinestone-covered high heels. "I've worn some tootsie tighteners in my day, but these are ridiculous. Is Uncle Sam trying to torture us or something?"

Jo turned from the mirror. "Hey, you guys are supposed to be wearing happy faces to prevent me from sinking into some kind of post-traumatic stress syndrome attack. Remember?"

"Oh yeah," Theresa said, readjusting the strap of her shoe. "I guess I'm just feeling a little bit nervous about pulling this whole thing off."

"If anyone guesses that we're not who we claim to be, we'll end up with our throats slashed faster than you can say 'Spy Girl to the rescue,'" Caylin agreed.

"Gee, thanks for the news flash." Jo headed out of the bathroom, Theresa and Caylin trailing behind.

"Seriously, Jo, how are you holding up?" Theresa asked as they entered the large master bedroom, where Jo had set up camp. "You look a little . . ."

"Pale," Caylin finished. "Do you feel all right?"

"Physically, I'm fine. Mentally . . . I've had better moments." Jo pulled a tiny sequined handbag out of her enormous closet.

She was usually totally pumped at times like this. The adrenaline would flow through her veins as she prepared for a mission, always expecting the unexpected. But tonight she was aware only of a vague sense of dread and the fact that a clump of mascara had wedged itself in the corner of her left eyelid.

Theresa paced back and forth across the lush green wall-to-wall carpeting that covered Jo's bedroom. "It's imperative that we all put aside our doubts," she said, stopping midstride. "We have to face tonight like it's any other night."

"Right," Caylin agreed. "If we don't force ourselves to rev up, this night is going to be a disaster."

There was no arguing the wisdom of Theresa and Caylin's words. Jo knew that her job allowed little room for excess emotional baggage. "I'll come through, Spy Chicks," she promised.

"We know you will," Caylin said. "You never have to doubt our faith in you."

"On that note, I think we need to get in a bit more dance practice before we descend upon El Centro," Theresa exclaimed. "Let's get ready to sambaaaa!"

## Dial "V" for Vengeance

Theresa turned on the stereo and tuned the radio in to a Brazilian salsa station. As the fast-paced music played, Jo demonstrated the groove for Theresa and Caylin. The heaviness she had felt earlier evaporated as Jo watched her friends struggling with the new dance steps.

"Your hips should move *naturally*," Jo explained. "You two look like you're being jerked around by a sadistic puppeteer." Losing herself in the music of her childhood, Jo continued to dance.

"I think I'm getting it!" Caylin yelled after a few minutes. "Samba, samba, samba." She moved across the carpet, swaying her hips as if she were in a music video.

"Great!" Jo laughed as she watched Caylin get into the Latin groove.

"How am I doing?" Theresa asked. She still looked as if she were dancing with a strait-jacket on.

"Uh . . . more hips." Theresa was never going to be able to put the samba on her dance resume, but Jo admired her effort.

"Like this?" Theresa thrust out her left hip. Too much. Her feet flew out from beneath her, and she landed on the carpet face first.

"Um, no, not exactly." Jo tried to hold back her giggles as she helped Theresa stand up.

But there was no stopping the laughter. First Jo, then Caylin, then Theresa gave in to a fit of hysteria.

"You better tell people dancing is against your religion," Caylin advised. "Otherwise we're going to get kicked out of the club as a health risk."

"I'll just stand to the side and look sultry." Theresa pouted her lips and let her eyelids droop. "Is this sexy?"

"We'll find out soon enough," Jo told her. "The witching hour has arrived."

They headed out to the Alfa Romeo, still giggling. "Drugs, money, beautiful clothes. I feel like I've walked into a movie about shallow twenty-somethings trying to quote unquote find themselves," Caylin commented as she slid into the car.

"Well, at least we look our parts," Jo said, getting behind the wheel. "We have never been hotter babes than we are right now."

"As long as my role doesn't require the samba, we'll all be up for Academy Awards," Theresa predicted.

Jo stepped on the gas. If it turned out that this informant could lead them to a drug lord, she could *guarantee* an Oscar-winning performance. "Next stop, El Centro."

*　　　*　　　*

"Talk about living out our lives as if we were on the set of a movie! This place is truly outrageous." Caylin had to shout over the music in order to communicate with her fellow Spy Girls. They were standing pressed against the bar, waiting for a round of non-alcoholic piña coladas from the oh-so-very-cute bartender.

Theresa gazed around the crowded club. "One thing is definite. Any gray-haired dude roaming around this place is going to be easy to spot."

"No kidding," Jo agreed. "I think we've walked into a Beautiful People's Anonymous group."

El Centro was packed with young men and women, all dressed to the hilt in outfits that looked as if they had sprung fully accessorized from the pages of *Vogue*. Caylin couldn't see anyone over the age of twenty-five in the whole place.

"Maybe our informant got spooked," Theresa suggested. "This could turn out to be nothing more than a night out on the town."

Jo picked up one of the large, frosty drinks the bartender had placed before them and took a long sip. "I have to admit that I'm starting to enjoy myself."

Caylin felt as if she were on the spring break

25

trip of the century. Pounding music, hot guys, tasty drinks . . . all sans parents. If it weren't for the fact that they were very possibly on an incredibly dangerous mission, this scenario would be too good to be true.

"I'd like to offer a suggestion," Jo announced, raising her drink.

"Be our guest," Caylin said. She wanted to hear what Jo had to say, but she also wanted to engage in flirtatious eye contact with a gorgeous blond guy who was dancing a few feet away from them. Oh, well. Who was to say she couldn't do both? "Proceed."

"I move that we split up, search for hotties, and enjoy ourselves," Jo suggested.

"What about the informant?" Theresa asked.

Jo shrugged. "If he's here, we'll find him."

Caylin glanced at the *Baywatch* babe to her left. "Jo's right. I mean, as long as we keep our eyes open for a geezer holding a red flower, I don't see what else we can do."

Theresa took a sip of her piña colada and stared off into space for a long moment, thinking. "Okay. But if we do spot someone who seems like he could be our informant, then we drop Operation Scam immediately."

"Of course," Jo agreed. "We'll do the beeper thing, then meet back here to consult before proceeding."

Caylin set her drink on the bar. "Happy hunting, girls." Without a backward glance, she glided toward the dance floor. The mission might be a bust, but if blondie was half as sweet as he looked, the night was going to be an unqualified winner.

"Baby, baby, baby . . . oh yeah, baby, baby, baby." Caylin sang slightly off-key to the pounding music.

She wasn't doing the samba, but her hips had definitely found a life of their own. Unfortunately, the blond had been a dud. But Caylin had discovered that dancing with herself was just as fun as the partner thing.

"You dance very well, pretty lady." A deep but oily voice interrupted her solo groove.

Caylin moved her head to take a gander at her new admirer. Yikes! He was older, and his hair the kind of salt-and-pepper look that was commonly referred to as "distinguished." Could it be?

"Hello," Caylin responded. "Um, are you looking for someone?"

"I think I've found her." His English was perfect, and the suit looked expensive. The man had definite informant possibilities.

"Tell me more." Caylin moved closer, her nerves jangling.

In a flash, the man's hands encircled Caylin's waist. He pulled her close, pressing his hips against hers and breathing hot, stale air into her ear. Yuck. This wasn't dancing; it was wrestling.

"Whoa, tiger," Caylin shouted over the music. "The forbidden dance really ain't my style."

"Ah, yes, I see the lovely girl is a bit shy." He winked and grabbed a long-stemmed silk rose from a small bud vase on a nearby table. "If you will allow me, I'll buy out an entire florist's shop and offer its contents to the lady who smells as sweet as a rose."

Ooh. Caylin had heard of going deep undercover. But this was beyond any superspy stuff she had ever seen. There was simply no way this Mr. Rourke look-alike was any kind of informant. He did, however, redefine the term *cheesy*. Exiting the situation seemed like a primo idea.

"Adios, amigo." Okay, so her limited Spanish wasn't Portuguese. At least she was *attempting* to blend. Caylin saluted Rico Suave and melted into the crowded dance floor. Next!

El Centro was brimming with guys who looked as if they might have at one point posed for *GQ*, but Jo couldn't focus on finding a hot Brazilian guy to show her the sights of Rio. Everywhere she looked, Jo saw possible informants. So what if their hair wasn't gray and there were no signs of a telltale red flower?

And there, by the bar, was another likely prospect. Aha. There was some actual gray hair on his head. Finally she was getting warmer. Jo sauntered toward the bar, rehearsing her opening line. Excuse me, sir, have you informed on any drug lords lately? Hey, dude, how about telling me what Rio is *really* about? Hmmm. Maybe a bit more subtlety was in order.

"Hey, there," Jo greeted her prey. "Come here often?" Okay, she wasn't going to win a lot of points for originality, but Jo thought her voice was sounding fairly smokin'. She would certainly get the guy's attention.

The gray-haired daddy stared at her in confusion. "Eh?"

Interesting. The man didn't speak English. Good thing Jo was the one who had spotted him. Caylin and Theresa would have been at a loss for words—literally.

"Are you looking for someone?" Jo asked in flawless Portuguese.

He nodded. "I'm meeting a woman here. But we've never met before." His eyes scanned the crowd as he spoke.

"Are you two going to have a *secret* rendezvous?" Jo asked, fluttering her lashes.

He raised his rather bushy gray eyebrows. "Secret? No."

Jo bit her lip, wondering how to proceed. The old dude wasn't jumping at her bait. Then again, a lot of people had a hard time digesting the notion that spies could be as young as the Trio Grande. She would push further.

"Do you have a flower to give me?" Jo whispered. "If so, we could go somewhere private and . . . uh . . . talk about it."

Mr. X frowned, squinting his bright green eyes at Jo. "Young lady, you are an affront to your generation."

"Uh, what?" Jo was accustomed to being described as one of those rare sterling examples of America's youth.

"I'm old enough to be your grandfather. These flirtatious comments are simply outrageous." He was getting more and more worked up as he spoke. Uh-oh. If the man had a heart attack, Jo had no one but herself to blame.

"Sorry, I, uh, didn't mean . . ." Her voice trailed off as she felt her face turning crimson. Flirting with a geezer—talk about mortification!

"You Americans don't know where to draw

the line!" the man finished. "Now go home and wash that revolting paint off your face." He pivoted away from Jo and strode toward the other side of the club.

Jo stared at the man's retreating back, wishing the floor would open up and swallow her. This night was going absolutely nowhere at the speed of light.

Theresa twirled a miniature parasol between her fingers and mentally recited the entire times table. She had been officially bored for over half an hour. Sure, the fellas here were oh-so-fine to *stare* at, but she hadn't had much success with actual conversation. The guys either didn't know how to speak English or were only interested in discussing various parts of her anatomy.

And there was *no* way Theresa was going to hit the dance floor. There weren't enough strobe lights in Brazil to make her dancing look anything but totally embarrassing. She had finally resorted to sitting at a tiny table, hoping against hope to catch sight of someone with gray-streaked hair and a red flower.

"I'll get another drink," Theresa said to her parasol. "Maybe a virgin strawberry daiquiri this time." The parasol didn't respond. Typical.

Theresa relinquished her chair, wondering how long spy protocol dictated that the trio hang out at El Centro. This pounding music was giving her a major headache. She glanced toward the source of the music, a large glass-enclosed DJ booth on the second level of El Centro. Huh. There was someone dancing in the window of the booth. Someone with gray-streaked hair and a red silk shirt.

Theresa squinted, staring at the booth. Wow. The hair was now obscured, but even from where she was standing, Theresa could make out that there was a flower pattern covering the shirt. Alert! Alert! This was not a test!

Theresa pulled her tiny ever present beeper from her small purse. "Sorry to interrupt your scamming, Spy Girls, but Trixie may have hit the jackpot."

"Are you sure you saw the informant?" Jo asked Theresa five minutes later. "Because I've had a few bum steers."

Theresa shrugged. "I'm not *sure*. I mean, I didn't charge up there and say, 'Hi, are you the anonymous informant I'm looking for?'"

"It does seem weird that the guy would be hanging out in the DJ booth," Caylin commented, glancing toward the large window.

It was empty. "Still, we might as well check it out."

"Gee, thanks for your confidence in my ability," Theresa responded. "I'm telling you, I saw gray-streaked hair and I saw a red flowered shirt."

"So what's the plan?" Caylin asked.

"I'll do the talking," Jo offered. "We don't know how much English the guy is going to know."

"Sounds good to me," Theresa responded. "I'll be ready with the mascara cam in case photos seem like a good idea."

"And I'll keep my eyes open for suspicious underworld types hanging around," Caylin said. "We have to be extra vigilant about possible traps."

"Wonder-triplet powers activate!" Jo said. "Let's get this thing over with."

The girls walked single file up the wrought iron staircase that led to the DJ booth. Caylin's heart hammered in her chest. If Theresa's instincts were correct, then the girls were about to start their mission for real. The idea was equal parts thrilling and terrifying.

At the top of the narrow flight of stairs, Jo knocked on a heavy, metal door. "I doubt anyone can even hear us in there."

"Unless the person inside is *waiting* for our arrival," Theresa pointed out.

Jo shrugged, then pounded on the door for several seconds. "I guess there's no one—"

Suddenly the door flew open. Caylin peered over Jo's shoulder, her heart thumping wildly. But the guy at the door didn't have gray-streaked hair. He was tall, cute, and very blond. The guy was also wearing a pair of huge headphones. Aha. The DJ.

"False alarm," Caylin said to Theresa over her shoulder. "But hey, I think we just found the best-looking guy in the place."

Then the guy moved aside, revealing a young woman who was sitting in a plush armchair. Caylin's eyes lit on her hair, which was very coifed and very black—aside from a two-inch-wide skunk streak straight down the middle. And yes, she was wearing a red flower-patterned shirt.

"False alarm?" Theresa whispered. "Doesn't look like it to me."

"Wow . . . he's a she," Jo said. She seemed powerless to walk into the booth and begin questioning this latest candidate. "And she's no older than we are."

The young woman stood up and walked toward the trio as the dude with the headphones retreated to the high-tech sound board lining one end of the small room. Skunk Chick didn't seem surprised that three American debutantes had arrived, unannounced, at the door of the DJ booth. In fact, she wore a welcoming smile.

"Congratulations," the stranger said in smooth, perfect English. "I see you've found me."

"Bingo," Caylin whispered.

**T**his mission is getting weirder by the second," Theresa whispered to Caylin. "Where are we *going?*"

The supposed informant was leading Theresa, Caylin, and Jo through a maze of hallways and tiny, hidden staircases. Apparently El Centro was constructed like a giant labyrinth.

Caylin shook her head. "I have no idea where she's taking us—I just hope there aren't any men with guns waiting for us at our destination."

At last the young woman stopped in front of a door. She began to usher the Spy Girls into a large, circular office that overlooked El Centro's large dance floor three stories below.

"Quickly," she ordered, grabbing Caylin's arm and pulling her inside the room.

Caylin raised her eyebrows at her fellow Bondettes as they watched their host dart around the spacious office. The young woman was gorgeous, but her olive-skinned face was lined with worry as she stared out the window, scanning the club.

"Is the place bugged?" Theresa whispered nervously.

The so-called informant was looking under the telephone and between the leaves of a plant sitting on the large glass desk that dominated one side of the room. After another minute of seemingly aimless searching, she closed all the window blinds.

"Do you want to frisk us?" Jo asked dryly.

The young woman took a seat in a black leather armchair and folded her hands across her lap. "Please . . . sit down," she responded, ignoring Jo's inquiry.

Caylin plopped onto a long sofa. "Don't worry, we would know if someone were observing us."

The young woman looked doubtful. "One can never be too careful."

"Are you satisfied that the coast is clear?" Theresa asked.

The so-called informant smiled. "Yes, I'm sure now. And I'm sorry to appear so paranoid . . . but I don't think I need to tell you what kind of stakes we're dealing with here."

"We're well aware that the stakes are high," Caylin answered quickly. There was no disputing *that* point.

"Good. Then we all understand each other."

Caylin was relieved that this girl—whoever she was—seemed as concerned with safety as the Spy Girls were. And she looked friendly. Caylin could usually spot a phony smile, but this one seemed genuine.

"I hope you are all enjoying your time in Rio," the young woman said calmly, as if the four of them had just sat down to participate in a tea party. "Our city offers many beautiful sights . . . not the least of which is our male population."

"So we've noticed," Jo answered.

Again the stranger's pretty face grew serious. "I'm thankful to all of you for being here—but I'm afraid I don't even know your names."

The Spy Girls exchanged a quick glance. Part of Caylin wanted to be totally honest with their paranoid hostess. She seemed completely sincere and trustworthy—but as the girl herself had stated, one could never be too careful. Jo nodded in silent agreement.

"I'm Jacinta," Jo said, extending her hand. "And my friends are Corinne and . . . uh, Trixie." She paused. "For now, I think first names are enough."

The stranger grinned. "And even those are not your real names, I presume?"

"What's your name?" Theresa asked, dodging the question.

"I am Diva—first name only." She paused. "Now, I am guessing that the three of you would like to know a little about my situation."

"That's why we're here," Jo confirmed. "Tell us everything you can."

Diva leaned forward in her chair and looked each of the Spy Girls in the eyes. "Drugs—and the crimes associated with drugs—have ruined my family," she said softly. "My father is in grave danger."

"Go on," Jo urged. "We're listening." Her face softened; clearly Diva's words were affecting her deeply.

"This club looks wonderful on the outside," Diva continued. "People dance, laugh, enjoy the drinks and the music." She stood up and walked to the window, then peered through the blinds. "You all feel safe here, yes?"

"Yeah," Caylin agreed. "However. I'm guessing there's a pretty major 'but' coming."

Diva nodded. "This place is actually filthy with crime. The big boss of the most powerful drug ring in Brazil oversees El Centro."

"Uh, wow . . ." Theresa glanced around the office, then back at Diva. "What does that mean—exactly?"

"Information about the drug trade comes in

and out of the club every single day. It's Underground Zero." Diva fell silent, allowing the girls time to absorb her statement.

Caylin felt yet another surge of adrenaline course through her veins. Could Diva be for real? If what she said was true, then all four of them were proverbial sitting ducks. And from the expressions on Theresa and Jo's faces, they were thinking the same thing.

"Should we really be sitting here discussing this, Diva?" The slight tremble in Jo's voice belied her calm exterior. "Frankly, it doesn't seem as if we should be here *period*."

"We have every right to be here," Diva countered. "This is my office."

"You work here?" Theresa asked.

Diva smiled. "I don't just work here. El Centro is mine. I own it."

Caylin sank into the cushions of the leather sofa. This new piece of information put an unexpected twist on the mission. Diva's information was certainly explosive—and more dangerous than Caylin had ever imagined.

"I say we pack our bags and head back to the States," Theresa suggested to her fellow Spy Girls. "Our training hasn't prepared us for anything this intense."

As soon as Diva had revealed that she

owned El Centro, Jo had asked her to step out of the office so the girls could converse in private. This thing was seriously sticky.

"What do you think, Cay?" Jo asked, although she already had a feeling that Caylin was going to jump on the let's-run-like-the-wind bandwagon.

Caylin frowned. "If everything Diva says is true, we can assume that she's in business with this drug lord. I don't know how much we can trust her as an informant."

"Her motives are seriously doubtful," Theresa added. "I mean, if this dude goes down, who knows what happens to El Centro?"

"Not to mention the fact that the club was very likely built with drug money," Caylin pointed out. "Diva owes her livelihood to the Big Boss."

Jo sighed. She couldn't refute anything that Theresa and Caylin had said. But there was something in Diva's eyes that Jo responded to. She had recognized Diva's pain and desperation, her fervent wish to extricate her family from the clutches of the drug trade.

"I think we should stay," Jo said firmly. "I haven't been in Diva's exact situation, but I know where she's coming from."

"I don't know, Jo. . . ." Theresa bit her lip. "I mean, Jacinta."

"Drugs and crime killed my own father. I know the anguish these people cause and the power they wield." Jo lowered her voice. "It's likely that Diva *can't* get out from under the hold of the Big Boss. Putting him in jail, where he can't hurt her family, is her only hope." She paused.

"In other words, *we're* her only hope," Caylin said.

"If we can help her bring down the drug lord, she can save her father and get her life back. If I were in her place, I would do whatever it took to accomplish that—no matter how dangerous it was." Jo was quiet as they all considered their dilemma.

"I guess we're going to have to give it a shot," Theresa said finally. "We'll do it in memory of Mr. Carreras."

"I'm in." Caylin walked to the door of the office. "Shall I invite Diva back inside?"

Jo nodded. Well, that was that. They would leave Brazil victorious—or in body bags.

Diva strode into the room and put her hands on her hips. "So? Will you help me?"

"We're all in this together now," Jo assured her. "We'll do whatever it takes."

"Thank you! Thank you so much." Diva beamed. "I don't know exactly who you girls are, but I'm glad you showed up."

"So what's next?" Caylin asked. "We need a plan—a good one."

Diva nodded. "To pull off an effective sting operation, our story has to be airtight."

"Here's the deal," Jo explained to Diva. "As far as you know, the three of us are filthy rich American debutantes, out to expand our fortune by getting into the drug trade."

"We're rebelling against our parents and lusting after a taste of the glamorous life," Theresa added excitedly. "We love danger, adventure—"

"I get the picture," Diva said with a laugh. "And I think it's a perfect cover. I mean, who but spoiled American brats would have access to so much cash?"

"Not *all* Americans are shallow," Caylin reminded Diva. "Some of us care about more than money."

"Well, luckily for us, money is the *only* thing the boss cares about." Diva took out a pad and pen and began to take notes. "Now, we must decide what kind of offer you girls will make."

"Um, ten thousand dollars?" Theresa suggested. "That should buy the Big Boss enough cocaine to theoretically ruin the lives of every member of a small town."

Diva snorted. "Ten thousand is small change

to these men, Trixie. I'm going to suggest that you offer him five hundred thousand dollars to start with."

Jo gasped. "Five hundred *thousand* dollars? Are we discussing American dollars?" She had never even conceived of that much money in one place at one time.

"Whoa . . . that's a lot of moolah," Caylin whispered. "Even for three rich debs."

"But Diva is right," Theresa said. "This man is probably used to trading millions of dollars' worth of cocaine at one time. If he's going to take us seriously as investors, we have to be in his league."

"Yes, now you understand." Diva smiled, her cheeks flushing. "If anyone questions the source of your income, you can say that you just came into the money from your trust funds, yes?"

Jo had to admire Diva. She was both smart and fearless—two of Jo's favorite qualities. For the first time, she began to feel confident about the mission. Thank goodness Diva thought the Big Boss would be interested in a straight cash investment. The trio wouldn't have to purchase drugs directly from anyone. Phew! Even if it was for a good cause, Jo didn't want to be on the receiving end of *any* amount of *anything* in the "this is your brain on" department.

"Half a mil it is," Jo said decisively. "What next?"

"I'll mention to the boss that you girls were around, looking to get into the business. I'll let him know that I have every reason to believe that working with you would be profitable."

"Do you think he'll bite?" Caylin asked.

Diva nodded. "The man is greedy. He won't let this opportunity pass him by."

"It's imperative that we meet with him personally," Jo said. "That's the only way we can ensure that the sting will work." She wasn't going to risk another lack-of-evidence case. Jo wanted to make a hundred percent sure that the creep got what was coming to him.

"I'm sure I'll be able to set up a meeting between you and the big boss . . . eventually," Diva allowed.

"What do you mean, 'eventually'?" Theresa asked.

"The man himself won't meet you face-to-face until you're approved by some of his underlings. If they give you the go-ahead, he'll invite you to his home."

"Underlings?" Jo pictured heavyset thugs with greasy hair and huge gold chains. Double gross.

Diva wiggled her eyebrows. "Believe me, that will be the most fun part of this adventure.

The guys who work for the boss are . . . well, extremely attractive. And they'll take you to the most happening places in Rio."

"Hmmm . . . sounds interesting," Caylin said. "Do they like blond Americans?"

"I don't need to remind you two that the guys in question are dangerous *criminals*," Theresa piped up. "There will be no romantic encounters. None."

Leave it to Theresa. "Absolutely. No romance. Now . . . do we have plan A?" Jo looked from her fellow spy girlies to Diva.

"Yes, it's a plan," Diva answered. "Shall we shake on it?"

As Jo gripped Diva's hand in her own, she uttered a silent prayer. They needed all the help they could get.

"What *time* is it at The Tower, anyway?" Theresa stifled a yawn as Caylin dialed Uncle Sam's private phone number.

"Who cares? Early, late . . . Uncle Sam never sleeps." Jo had kicked off her high heels and was stretched out on one of the luxurious oriental rugs that covered the floor of the living room.

"Kind of like us," Theresa commented. The short nap she had taken on the plane seemed a lifetime ago. But the girls wanted to share their information with Uncle Sam before they retired to their rooms. Staying in close and constant touch with The Tower was their best safety guard.

"Good evening, Spy Girls." Uncle Sam's voice came over the speakerphone. "Were you successful tonight?"

Caylin leaned toward the phone. "We met with the informant. She seems to be on the level."

"And you all agree on that score?" Uncle Sam asked. "One can never be too careful."

The girls giggled. "That's exactly what she said," Theresa told him.

There was a pause. "So the informant is a female. Interesting."

"You're not going sexist on us, are you?" Jo asked him.

He laughed—a rarity. "Never, Jo. Never."

"There's one thing," Caylin said hesitantly. "We're going to need five hundred g's—in cash."

"I expected as much. Consider it done."

Theresa could practically hear the wheels turning in Uncle Sam's mind. Get cash. Transport cash to Rio. Contact backup agents. Et cetera. Et cetera.

"Thanks, Uncle Sam—we knew we could count on you." Jo's voice caught in her throat.

"We don't want anything to happen to screw up this mission."

"Nor do I," Uncle Sam responded. "Now get some sleep—and stay safe."

Caylin hung up the phone and leaned into the plush cushions of one of the living room's three sofas. "That's that. We've got the green light."

"So we proceed to the next stage," Theresa announced. "Operation Bring Down the Big Boss."

"Operation Revenge," Jo commented. "When I see this guy heading to the clinker, I'm going to look up to heaven and smile."

"But this guy isn't the one who killed your father, Jo," Caylin reminded her. "You can't make this mish only about personal vendettas. It's too dangerous."

"Missions are *always* personal," Jo corrected her. "If they weren't, the three of us wouldn't be willing to risk our lives over and over again."

Theresa nodded. They all had their reasons for wanting to fight evil in the world. But this mission . . . this mission belonged to Jo.

t the *Co*-pa! Copa-ca-baaa-naaa!" Caylin had sung the song a hundred times, but the lyrics had never been so appropriate. It was Saturday night, and the trio was safely stashed in the Alfa Romeo, driving toward the location of their all-important first meeting with Mr. X's business operatives.

"I'm psyched Diva is going to come along on this rendezvous. I love you two, but it's nice to have someone different around." Theresa leaned forward from the backseat and looked from Jo to Caylin. "Know what I mean?"

"Yep." Jo turned off the radio, causing Caylin's insistent humming to be the only sound in the car. "I sort of wish we could make Diva an honorary Spy Girl. The chick defines cool."

"I couldn't believe those dances she was showing us," Caylin said. "I think I actually got the hang of that slow, slow, fast thing." She paused. "Or is it fast, fast, slow?"

"Maybe we'll get to samba tonight," Jo suggested. "I could use a little dancing to lighten my mood."

"You'll find out soon enough." Theresa pointed to the hand-drawn map Diva had given them that afternoon. "According to this, we take a left here. The place is down the street."

"I hope it's crowded," Caylin said, peering into the dark night. "I mean, these guys can't just *kill* us with hundreds of people around—can they?"

"They won't *want* to kill us," Theresa assured her. "There's no way they'll figure out who we really are."

"I just wish we knew the Big Boss's name," Jo said. "If Diva would give us a positive ID, we could have Uncle Sam do a background check."

"You heard her," Caylin responded. "She's dead set against telling us the guy's name until we meet him face-to-face. According to her, we'll be safer that way."

Jo swung the Alfa Romeo to the left, then slowed to a stop. "I can't believe the restaurant is actually called La Americana," she commented. "Who knew we'd find such a home away from home?"

"Personally, I hope the *food* isn't American. I'm not in the mood for sunlamp burgers or cardboard pizza," Theresa commented as they got out of the sports car. "But I have to say, this place looks pretty darn empty of *americanas*—"

"As well as everyone of every *other* nationality, for that matter," Caylin finished. "Hey, look—there's a sign on the door."

"What's it say?" Theresa asked.

Jo led her *compadres* up to La Americana's front door and squinted through the darkness at the sign. "Uh-oh," Jo said. "The sign says the place is closed for a private party."

"Maybe we're at the wrong place," Caylin suggested.

"Or we have the wrong day," Theresa said. She took a few steps away from the door and glanced around the near empty parking lot.

"Great!" Jo kicked the door in frustration. "This isn't exactly the auspicious start I was hoping for."

The door opened. Standing on the other side of it was one of the hottest guys Caylin had ever seen. Jet black hair, coal black eyes, deeply tanned skin. Yum, yum.

"Ah, you ladies are right on time," the guy said with just about the sexiest accent Caylin had ever heard.

"W-we are?" Theresa asked. "I mean, yes, of *course* we are."

"Diva arrived a few minutes ago," Señor

Hottie continued. "She has assured us that we will all have a marvelous time this evening."

"I guess we're the private party," Theresa whispered as Jo introduced herself to their host in Portuguese.

Señor Hottie was bent over Jo's hand. An actual, real-live, old-school kiss on the hand took place right before Caylin's eyes.

"Jacinta, I am pleased to make your acquaintance."

It was incredibly hard to believe that this heartthrob was also a cold-blooded drug trader. If nothing else, his manners were exquisite.

"And who are you?" Jo asked flirtatiously.

"I am Juan." He turned to Theresa. "And you must be Trixie."

"Pleased to meet you," Theresa said, extending her hand.

He looked into Caylin's eyes. "And you, my dear, are Corinne." Yeow. If Juan's fellow operatives were half as cute as *he* was, the girls were going to have to work *mighty* hard to keep their minds on the mission.

"Shall we go inside?" Juan asked.

"Let the games begin," Jo said.

The Spy Girls exchanged glances, then followed Juan into La Americana . . . where their fate awaited them.

\*　　\*　　\*

Theresa shut her eyes in order to *truly* savor the succulent beef dish that had been served as the third course. Boy, the SG's dinner companions sure gave new meaning to the expression "wine and dine." In addition to three different beef dishes, the table was laden with roast duck, stuffed lobster, and a melt-in-your-mouth cheese soufflé. Yummy! Theresa had never felt so pampered by a member of the male population—or by *any* member of the population, for that matter.

"You enjoy your meal, yes?" inquired Carlos, Theresa's de facto date for the evening.

She nodded and popped another piece of the thinly sliced beef into her mouth. "It's delicious."

"I'll never be able to look at a duck again . . . without wanting to eat it for dinner," Caylin commented.

"I know what I would like for *dessert*." That charming comment had come from Caylin's so-called date, Jorge.

Yeah, these guys were laying on the compliments so thick, Theresa could have cut them with a knife. And yes, they were largely relying on thousand-dollar suits and gourmet food to impress the girls. But Theresa had to admit that their tactics worked. She felt totally swept up in the glamour of the evening. Jeez, one of the best big bands in all of Rio—according to Diva, who *obviously* knew about such things—was playing just for the eight of them.

Life didn't get much sweeter than this—as long as Theresa didn't dwell too much on the fact that all of these guys were probably packing heat underneath their Prada suits. That notion had a really annoying way of bringing Theresa's giddiness meter down a few notches.

As two tuxedoed waiters circled the table, setting down tiny cups of espresso in front of each of them, Armand cleared his throat.

"Let us talk for a moment, ladies," he said. "Then we can delight in the rest of the evening."

It had been clear from the start that Armand was the leader of this merry band. And Theresa's initial speculation had been confirmed earlier by Diva. While the two girls were reapplying lipstick in the bathroom, Diva had whispered to Theresa that Armand was *the* man to impress.

Theresa had passed along that tidbit of information to Jo, who had spent every minute since beguiling Armand. So far, Jo's performance had been a roaring success. No surprises there.

"Trixie, Corinne, and I are extremely

anxious to explore the many opportunities that Rio has to offer," Jo purred as she sat back from the table and ran the tip of her index finger around the rim of her espresso cup. Flawless. Even *Theresa* was having a difficult time remembering that she and her compatriots weren't actually three debs looking for action.

"Yes, Brazil is a country filled with possibilities," Armand responded. "Of course, one has to have money—and spend money—in order to *make* money."

"So true," Caylin said. "Equally, it's important that we know *where* to spend that money."

"Which is why we're all here tonight," Diva broke in. "These young women are serious about exploring the options you have to offer."

"And what is the *extent* to which you three wish to explore?" Armand asked. He looked at each Spy Girl in turn, his eyebrows raised.

This was it. The Offer. Make-it-or-break-it time. Theresa held her breath as she waited for Jo to respond. She also offered silent thanks that Jo had become their designated spokeswoman. Theresa didn't think she would have been able to get the giant figure to roll off her tongue without gagging.

"On a scale of one to a million . . . we're at

about five hundred thousand," Jo said calmly. "I'm referring to our level of interest, naturally."

Armand grinned, then bowed his head. "Naturally." He paused. "Now tell me, Jacinta, what sort of benefits are you all hoping to derive from . . . exploring your options?"

"At some point in the near future, we would like to see our money *grow*. We don't need to *see* the growth. . . . We just want to pick the fruit off the tree."

Theresa was tempted to applaud. Who knew that Jo was a master of veiled language? She sounded so *professional*. It was almost eerie.

Armand raised his espresso cup. "I think that our boss will be very interested in assisting you ladies in your quest for opportunity. Cheers."

There was an echo of cheers around the table. Glasses clinked, lips smiled, a couple of people giggled. As the hot, rich espresso warmed Theresa's stomach, she snuck a glance at Diva, who was seated next to Juan.

"You're in," Diva mouthed silently.

"We are done with business, yes?" Armand asked the girls.

"Yes," Caylin confirmed.

"Then let's party!" Armand stood up and

turned toward the band. "Tonight—we samba!"

The evening had lulled Jo into a kind of satisfied stupor. As she listened to the big band's seductive tunes, Jo felt herself mentally slipping further and further away from the implications of this dangerous mission. For this moment, at least, she was nothing more than a young woman out for a good time. She closed her eyes, enjoying the sensation of Armand's arms around her waist as they danced.

"I have always felt American ladies were . . . how do you say . . . beneath me. But you are very beautiful," Armand said, his voice suggestive.

Talk about a backhanded compliment! Jo wanted to rebuke Armand for his rather out-moded attitude, but he was simply too gorgeous to resist. His dark eyes gave new meaning to the term *come hither.*

"You're not so bad yourself," Jo murmured. "I could dance all night."

"Ah, yes, but I have other activities in mind." Armand's voice was silky, his hands warm and insistent on her back.

"You do?" Jo knew she wasn't supposed to allow either romance or lust to cloud her objective. She'd made *that* mistake before—twice. But getting in good with the Big Boss's yes-men was a key aspect of their mission. She was practically *obligated* to flirt up a storm.

Armand pulled Jo even closer, then lowered his lips to hers. The kiss was sensual, soft, everything a kiss should be. At first. Then Armand pressed his body firmly against Jo's . . . and she felt cold, hard metal pressing against her ribs.

A gun. Reality came crashing down. This wasn't a romantic evening with a hot guy. This was the beginning of an elaborate sting operation designed to put these guys—and their boss—in jail. Armand had a gun, and Jo had no doubt that he would be willing to use it, no matter how polite his manners were over dinner and drinks.

Images flashed through Jo's mind. That steel gun pressed against her father's head. The vivid colors that had been spattered all over her white shirt—

Jo jerked out of Armand's arms. "No, no." Her breathing was ragged as Armand's face seemed to metamorphose into the face of her father's killer. A face she'd never forgotten.

"Jacinta, what is the matter?" Armand sounded irritated, as if he couldn't imagine why

someone of the female gender would so will-
ingly, *forcefully* step out of his embrace.

"I just, um, have to go," Jo told him. Her
stomach was churning, and she felt as if faint-
ing were a distinct possibility.

Without a glance at Theresa or Caylin, Jo
fled. Right now, she simply had to be alone.

Uh-oh. Jo had just freaked out—big time.
Caylin tore her attention away from Jorge and
watched Jo flee the dance floor.

"What is wrong with her?" Armand
shouted. "She is like a crazy woman!"

Caylin gave Jorge an apologetic smile and
slid out of his embrace. Out of the corner of
her eye, she saw that Theresa was flashing
Carlos a similar worried grin. It was official.
They were facing a crisis.

"I demand to know what is going on!"
Armand yelled.

For the first time that night, it was easy to
believe that Armand was a powerful, dangerous, *vicious* man with a criminal mind.
Caylin felt the hairs on the back of her neck
rise as she stared at Armand's reddening face.
Yikes. She wouldn't want to be on *his*
bad side.

"Why does she react this way to my kiss?"
Armand demanded.

She had to think fast. Very fast. "Um . . . she has a boyfriend?" Caylin offered.

Armand's face went from bright red to dark purple in three seconds flat. "Jacinta is a tease. How can she behave that way with me if she has a boyfriend? It is shameful!"

Caylin shot a significant glance at Diva, who slipped out of Juan's arms and headed off toward where Jo had made her impromptu exit. Thank goodness for their new friend. If anyone had the wherewithal to get Jo back on track right now, it would be her. In the meantime, it was up to "Corinne" and "Trixie" to try and soothe Armand's hackles, which were really, uh, *hackling*.

"Hey, Trixie, want to help me out here?" Caylin whispered out of the side of her mouth.

Theresa put a hand on Armand's shoulder and gave him a sympathetic squeeze. "The thing is, Jacinta is thinking about breaking up with her boyfriend. I mean, he's, like, totally mean to her. She doesn't like him at all."

Armand narrowed his eyes. "Where is he? I will kill him!"

Oops. Theresa's heart was in the right place, but provoking Armand's macho side probably wasn't the best idea under the circumstances.

Caylin stepped forward. "Listen, Armand, it's like this. . . ."

As Caylin babbled on, she prayed that Diva would be able to calm Jo down. If this mission was going to be a success, they had to play their hand carefully. And unless Jo came back for some major damage control, the Big Meeting with Armand's Big Boss could very well get called off—and the mission would be a Big Bust. Or worse.

**J**o?" Diva called from the other side of the bathroom door. "May I come inside?"

Jo quickly wiped the tears from her cheeks and took several deep, calming breaths. "Uh, sure," she answered weakly.

The door opened, and Diva slipped into the luxurious bathroom. She perched beside Jo on the red velvet settee and placed a comforting arm around her shoulders.

"Is there anything I can do?" Diva asked.

Jo sniffed. "Don't you even want to know why I ran off like a maniac?"

Diva shrugged. "I know what it is like to have dark shadows in one's life. Sometimes . . . well, sometimes the ghosts come out of the corners and one cannot fight them."

Jo couldn't have said it better herself—and Diva was speaking in her second language. "You and I have a lot in common," Jo said, brushing away one last tear. "My family was also torn apart by drugs."

Now it was Diva's turn to get weepy. "Sometimes I lie awake at night and imagine my life so differently. I picture myself and my family on a simple picnic, or going to church, or making dinner in the kitchen . . . all without the dark cloud of the *business* hanging over our heads."

"I don't understand why there's so much evil in the world." Jo rose from the settee and walked to a vanity table at the other side of the large bathroom. "When I was a little girl, my father protected me from that evil. But as I grew older, he taught me to fight it."

"Your father sounds like a wise man," Diva said.

Jo nodded. "He was."

"He passed away?" Diva asked. Her voice was hesitant, as if she were worried that her questions were getting too personal.

"Yes. He . . ." He was murdered. All because the justice system he loved had been corrupted by the drug trade.

"You don't have to tell me about it," Diva said softly. "I know how difficult it is to talk about these things."

In the reflection of the mirror over the vanity table, Jo saw Diva's face grow dark. "You obviously have your own tragedies to deal with," she said.

Diva sighed. "My hair used to be beautiful—it was a shiny, midnight black."

"It's still beautiful." Jo decided against pressing further. If Diva wanted to talk, she would.

"This—" She pointed to the stripe in her hair. "It hasn't always been there."

"No?" Now Jo's curiosity was uncontainable. "How did it get that way?"

"Part of my hair turned white the day my father—" Her voice broke, and she began to sob. They were the kind of deep, tearless sobs that tore apart one's insides.

Diva had appreciated Jo's privacy. Now Jo would return the favor. In time, she would probably discover the haunting secrets of Diva's past. Diva would tell her—when she was ready to.

"We're going to get this guy, Diva." In the mirror Jo's eyes locked with her new friend's.

Diva smiled weakly. "Yes. You three are my angels. You are going to help me and my family get our lives back."

"And you're going to help. Like I said, we're all in this together." Jo looked at herself in the mirror again and found that she was smiling. As always, Jo found that once the Spy Girl inside her focused all her negative energy on the mission, she felt completely energized. Jo knew what she had to do—now for Diva as much as for herself. This mission was about justice for all.

Jo stood up and faced Diva. "Shall we go back to the party?"

Diva executed a small but graceful curtsy. "By all means."

The two touched hands for a brief moment, then left the bathroom, ready to grapple with their fears.

"You are like fire that is made of liquid," Carlos exclaimed as Caylin was twirled around for what felt like the thousandth time.

"No, she is like fire that spits!" Jorge claimed as he grabbed Caylin and dipped her close to the floor.

Caylin knew that people got carsick and seasick. But was it possible to become dance sick? Jo and Diva's abrupt departure had created a dearth of females in the crowd. So for almost half an hour now, Theresa and Caylin had been juggling two guys each—both on *and* off the dance floor.

"This is great, guys, but I think Trixie needs a turn on the floor now." Caylin was panting, and her hair felt as if it were plastered against her sweaty forehead.

"Trixie is *on* the floor," Theresa called from a few feet away. "Oh, and *please* forget that I *ever* said I wanted to learn the samba."

Juan pulled Theresa close, then picked her up and spun her around several times. "Trixie says she is not good at the Latin dance, but we prove her wrong!"

Caylin gaped at Theresa. Was this the same girl whose idea of an ideal evening was surfing the web for chat rooms? Theresa's dress was slipping off her shoulders, and her brown hair was swinging wildly around her face.

"Corinne, we must show Trixie and Juan how much better *we* are on the floor, ah?" Armand had approached Caylin from behind. Without warning, he put his hands around her waist, then scooped her into his arms.

Well, at least Armand's nose had been wrestled back into its joint. Theresa and Caylin had fawned over him enough so that he seemed to have forgotten all about Jo's poorly timed freak-out. But enough was enough. If she and Theresa had to keep up this frenetic pace much longer, they weren't going to be able to get out of bed in the morning—much less work to bring down a drug lord.

"Whoaaa . . . !" Theresa cried. She slipped out of Juan's grasp and was now careening toward Armand and Caylin on her stilettos. "Watch out!"

*Smack!* Theresa had plowed into Caylin, causing a three-body pileup on the dance floor.

71

"I think I'm going to die," Theresa moaned.

Caylin remained on the brick floor, thankful for a moment of rest, no matter how ill-gotten. And then . . . a light at the end of the tunnel. Diva and Jo were heading toward them, arm in arm.

"Why do I feel like I just walked into an episode of *The Gong Show*?" Jo asked wryly, nearing the scene of the dance catastrophe.

Diva laughed. "Clearly we were missed out here."

"You have *no* idea." Caylin grabbed Jorge's outstretched hand and struggled to her feet.

"I think Trixie and Corinne need to hang up their pearls for the night," Jo said to Diva. "They're tough to be around if they don't get their beauty sleep."

"Gotcha." Diva placed her hand on Armand's shoulder and flashed him a flirtatious smile. "Armand, you gorgeous man, let's talk."

As if on cue, Jorge, Carlos, and Juan melted into the background. As the guys plunked into chairs around the dinner table, Theresa, Caylin, and Jo huddled.

"Do you think everything went according to plan?" Caylin asked. If the answer to that question was no, she had sacrificed both her feet and her equilibrium for no good reason.

"I think so," Jo answered. "Well, I *hope* so. Sorry for the glitch, guys. You know I didn't mean to let you down."

"You didn't," Theresa assured her. "Besides, your absence meant that Corinne and I got to suck up all the male attention for once."

Jo didn't respond, and Caylin realized that she was listening in on the conversation—strictly Portuguese—that was taking place between Diva and Armand. Their voices were hushed, and Caylin couldn't determine the tone of what was being said.

"Do you think it's a go?" Caylin whispered to Theresa.

"I think we're about to find out," Theresa whispered back. "They're heading this way."

Jo flashed a thumbs-up. "The news is going to be good," she promised, turning back to Caylin and Theresa.

"It has been a most wonderful evening," Armand announced. "But alas, the hour is late."

Instantly Jorge, Carlos, and Juan popped up from their seats and gravitated toward the girls. There seemed to be some kind of silent communication between the guys that dictated their actions. Did that mean a simple flick of Armand's wrist could result in one of Caylin's dance partners sticking a gun in her face?

"The pleasure has been ours, Armand," Jo said smoothly. "Please forgive my fit of emotion earlier. It's just that . . . I find you very attractive. So strong . . . so . . ." Jo let her words linger suggestively, then fluttered her lashes. "It was a moment of weakness."

Caylin suppressed a wince. She knew Jo was merely working on Armand's delusional side, but . . . *ugh.*

Armand looked gratified. He shrugged. "It is no problem. I know women—these things happen." He paused, glancing around the group to make sure he had everyone's attention. "My new friends, I would like to tell you that I am going to do my best to set up a meeting between you and our boss. As we discussed, he has many *investment* opportunities to offer."

It was the longest speech of the night—and apparently the last. Without another word, Armand and his cronies filed out of La Americana's back patio and disappeared into the dark night.

"Congratulations, amigas," Diva said with a smile. "You're in business."

Theresa was beyond exhaustion, but she knew that she would lie awake for a long time before she fell asleep tonight. The events of the last few hours whirled in her brain as she listened to Caylin and Jo brief Uncle Sam on the all-important evening.

"I'm very pleased with the progress you've made," Uncle Sam was saying. "I didn't want to undermine your confidence, but to tell you the truth, I wasn't at all sure that these men would agree to give three young American women the opportunity to meet with their boss."

"Great. Now you tell us." Sometimes Theresa appreciated the way Uncle Sam let them find out whether or not a mission was a go on their own. Other times, she wished he would take a slightly more hands-on approach.

"If the rest of the mission goes as well as tonight, then this Big Boss—whoever he is—can look forward to spending the rest of his life in the ole hoosegow." The satisfaction in Caylin's voice was evident. Already each of the girls had poured her soul into their latest adventure.

"So what are our chances of making it out of this thing alive?" Theresa asked.

"The Tower is prepared to back you up every step of the way," Uncle Sam assured them. "We can offer you a suitcase full of cash at a moment's notice."

"Cash is all well and good," Theresa responded.

"But I think I'd like a bullet-proof vest, thank you very much. Or maybe a force field. Can you whip that up for me, Sammo?"

"Just sit tight, Theresa." Uncle Sam was using his patronizing I-know-everything-there-is-to-know-about-international-espionage voice. "A veritable army of Brazilian and United States agents are on twenty-four-hour call. When you need the team behind you, they'll be there."

Caylin sat up a little straighter. "Whoa. That sounds so official."

"It *is* official. Each of these men and women has received special training in order to maximize the effectiveness of their actions while minimizing any risk of bodily harm."

Theresa noted that the term *bodily harm* sounded significantly less clinical when applied to *her* body. Her pain threshold was high—but not *that* high.

"I'm just relieved everything turned out okay tonight," Jo said with a deep sigh. "I can't believe I flaked." She had told Uncle Sam about her "little moment," but he had assured her that sometimes it happened to even the best spies.

"There was no harm done, Jo, I assure you," Uncle Sam soothed. "But I *am* wondering what went down at the end of the night."

"Their convo was all in Portuguese," Caylin informed him. "I couldn't understand a word."

"Jo, were you able to hear what Diva said to this man Armand? Was it something to allay any of his remaining fears or questions about associating with you three?" Uncle Sam asked.

"Sort of," Jo replied. "Basically Diva said, 'Just get them set up. . . . It'll all be over soon, anyway.'"

Theresa frowned. "Doesn't that sound just a tiny bit suspicious?" she asked the group at large. "I mean, I'm not thrilled with the idea of us being so-called set up."

"Diva is on the level," Jo insisted. "I'm as positive about that as I am about my own dress size."

Uncle Sam cleared his throat, interrupting Jo's defense of Wonder Diva. "Let's not speculate too much. It's safer to act based on what we know. And what we know is that everything is going according to plan. At least for now."

"Amen to that," Caylin piped up.

"Get some rest, you three. You're going to need all of your strength." With that, Uncle Sam hung up with his usual lack of the niceties.

Jo reached over and squeezed Theresa's

77

shoulder. "Don't worry, T. Diva's a stand-up chick. Like we said earlier, she could practically be a Spy Girl herself."

She was right. Diva had all of the qualities that made a good spy. She was smart, she was likable, and she had an innate ability to lie through her teeth. And *that* was what made Theresa so worried.

Caylin didn't want to open her eyes. She was in the middle of a particularly delicious dream starring herself, the lead hunk from the daytime soap *Pacific Sundown*, and a long, white, sandy beach. There was also a certain amount of suntan lotion being bandied about. Mmmm . . . Unfortunately, someone was pounding on her head. Wait, no. It wasn't her head. It was the door. Somebody was banging—loudly—on the front door of the mansion.

Caylin pried open her eyes and slid out of bed. She grabbed the fluffy terry cloth bathrobe hanging on the back of her bedroom door and stumbled into the hallway. From the other bedrooms, she heard the sounds of Theresa and Jo's soft snores. Lucky girls—probably still dreaming about superhotties of their own.

"I'm coming!" Caylin yelled as the pounding continued unabated. "And if you're selling magazines, we don't want any."

79

Caylin stumbled, still half asleep, to the bottom of the staircase. Now that she was at least semiconscious, she realized that this was one of those moments when a Spy Girl was wise to exercise caution. *Anybody* could be on the other side of that door. Then again, if someone really meant to burst in and slit her throat, he probably wouldn't announce his presence with such a flourish.

"Who is it?" Caylin called.

"I am Rocky," a guy called back. Okay, that was sort of a weird Brazilian name, but hey, what did she know?

"Uh, what do you want, Rocky?" Caylin asked. At least he spoke English—dealing with that pesky language barrier was a struggle she wasn't up for this early in the morning.

"I have an important message, miss. Please open the door." He sounded harmless enough. Brutal killers didn't usually say "please."

Caylin opened the door and tried to look as dignified as possible, considering the fact that she was wearing a bathrobe and fuzzy bunny slippers. "Yes?"

Rocky's eyes flickered down to her feet, then snapped back up to her face. He nodded formally. "My boss has requested the presence of Miss Corinne, Miss Trixie, and Miss Jacinta for lunch this afternoon." Ah. Rocky was obviously yet another emissary of the Big Boss. "He has business issues to explore with you."

"Will we be meeting your boss face-to-face, then?" Caylin asked. Her heart began to hammer within her chest as she realized that this might be It.

"A car will pick you up at one o'clock," Rocky said, ignoring her question. "Good day."

"Wait—," Caylin called. Where was the meeting taking place? How long would it last? Should they bring the money? She had a million questions, but Rocky was already jogging toward a large black Cadillac parked in the circle drive.

"I guess that wasn't an invitation," Caylin said softly, to no one but the grandfather clock in the front hall. "It was an order."

At 1:15 P.M. Jo sat in the back of the longest stretch limousine she had ever seen. The black leather interior was decked out with a TV, a high-tech stereo, and even a full wet bar. She felt like a cross between Princess Anne and a rock star's girlfriend. The girls were definitely traveling in style. And they were dressed to the proverbial nines. Each girl had picked out her best "power" suit and a strand of real pearls. Hello, Rodeo Drive!

"I hope our lunch is *satisfying*," Caylin commented, breaking the silence.

"Our host will probably be quite . . . uh, something," Theresa said, glancing at Jo.

Jo leaned back against one of the windows so that she could get a better look at the driver. Unlike most of the guys they had dealt with, the driver wasn't incredibly young and hot. He was more of a grandfather type—hopefully a grandfather who was losing his hearing.

Jo tapped on the glass. "Do you know where we're going?" she loudly asked the driver in Portuguese.

"Lunch," he answered in the same language, and Jo passed the news back to the peanut gallery.

"Do you think it's okay to *talk?*" Caylin wondered aloud.

Jo shrugged at Caylin and Theresa. "A lot of people in Brazil speak English," she said pointedly. "So if we *talk,* maybe we should include them in our conversation. Would you like that?"

"This sucks," Theresa whispered. "I feel like we're lambs being led to the slaughter."

"Well, let's be quiet lambs," Caylin suggested.

Jo agreed. Even if the driver couldn't understand their conversation, it was very possible that the Big Boss had his limo bugged. And Jo wasn't about to blow the whole mission because the three of them couldn't keep their mouths shut for a short car ride.

For several minutes the back of the limo was quiet except for Caylin's whistled rendition of "Don't Cry for Me, Argentina." The tension was mounting by the second. At last the driver cleared his throat.

"Here we are, ladies," the driver announced in perfect English a few minutes later, parking the car on a deserted residential street.

Oops. Good thing they hadn't blathered on about the mission. Spy Girl Lesson Number 402: Assume everyone speaks English.

As the trio climbed out of the car, Jo stared at their luncheon spot in shock. If this was the Big Man's house, he wasn't doing as well as they all thought. Yeah, the house was on the large side. And certainly the porch wasn't sagging and the roof tiles weren't falling off. But the place was hardly a palace. The girls' HQ was way ritzier. Like, about a hundred times way ritzier.

"Somehow I don't think there's an indoor pool here," Theresa whispered to Jo as they walked up the path to the front door.

"What's going on?" Caylin hissed. "I'm getting a bad feeling about this friendly little lunch."

Jo forced herself to smile brightly in case

someone was watching them from inside the modest home. "Well, it's too late to back out now."

The front door opened before they had a chance to knock. Standing on the other side was a pleasant-looking man in his late sixties. White hair, a small potbelly . . . this was Grandpa Number 1. He looked even older than the driver. Jo suddenly felt extremely conspicuous in her hot pink Chanel suit and matching pumps. Grandpa was wearing a cheap-looking seersucker suit and a pair of eyeglasses that looked as if they had been purchased circa 1965.

Jo was positive that Caylin and Theresa were thinking exactly what she was. Was it possible—at *all*—that the mild-mannered man standing before them was the Big Boss?

"Hello, girls!" he greeted them enthusiastically in English. "Corinne, Jacinta, Trixie, it is a pleasure to make your acquaintance."

Enough with the polite salutations already. Jo was ready for some *action*. "Hello, sir."

He smiled. "Please, call me Chico. All my friends do, yes, you understand?" He stepped away from the door and ushered the trio into the house.

Jo studied their surroundings as she followed Chico—whose walk bore a distinct resemblance to a duck's waddle—down a short hallway. The house wasn't ostentatious, to say the least, but it was clear that the people who lived there took great care to make the place homey and comfortable. There was children's artwork on the walls, crocheted throw rugs on the floor, and antique clocks tucked into many of the corners.

"Thank you for having us to lunch, uh, Chico," Theresa said as they walked into a small, cozy dining room. "This is quite an honor."

"The honor was ours," Chico responded, beaming from behind his thick eyeglasses. Okay, his English wasn't superb. But he had said "ours."

*Ours.* That could mean only one thing. Jo fully expected the Big Boss to emerge from another room with a sack full of white powder. Okay, maybe not the sack—the girls were strictly playing investor. But she at least expected to see The Man Himself at long last.

"You eat, yes?" Chico gestured toward a table laden with delicious-looking home-cooked food.

Jo could practically feel the pounds collecting on her hips. She exchanged glances with her fellow SGs as they took their seats around the table.

"Is anyone else joining us?" Caylin asked after an awkward moment of silence.

"Eat, eat," Chico said. He gestured toward the food, grinning and smacking his lips. "Is good, yes?"

Okay, it was beyond obvious that this guy wasn't the Big Boss. There was just no way. It was also obvious that he wasn't going to impart any information that he didn't feel was absolutely necessary.

"You heard our host," Theresa said firmly. "Let's eat."

Chico sat down at the head of the table and piled his plate high with rice, beans, and beef. After a few minutes of enjoying his meal, he patted his chin with a white linen napkin.

"So, you tell me your plan, yes?" He looked from one girl to the next, awaiting their response.

Jo considered responding in Portuguese, then decided against it. Letting Chico believe that none of them spoke his native language could turn out to be an advantage. One never knew what kind of conversations one might overhear. . . .

"We have half a million dollars of disposable income," Jo said, getting right to the point. "We would like to . . . make an investment."

"Ah, yes, wonderful, wonderful." Chico beamed at them, but it wasn't clear whether or not he had understood a word of what Jo had said. The expression on his face was somewhere between "addled professor" and "beatific monk."

Covert mission or no covert mission, this situation was beginning to border on the absurd. "Um, can you tell us what our next step is?"

Understanding flashed in Chico's electric blue eyes. "Yes, yes, soon," he responded. "Things take time, yes?"

Jo sighed. Talk about frustrating! The waiting was nothing short of excruciating. She would feel that way even if she really *were* a rich debutante looking to get into the drug business. Jo Carreras was *not* one to appreciate being lopped off on some dough-brained underling. She wanted to meet the Big Boss!

"No worry, Jacinta," Chico continued. "I think the boss like your plan, yes? You will meet him very soon. Very soon."

Jo took another bite of her black beans. That meeting better be worth the wait. She was beginning to feel as if the Spy Girls were playing an elaborate game of cat and three blind mice.

\*　　　\*　　　\*

El Centro was a totally different place during the day. Theresa couldn't believe this was the same club the girls had visited their first night in Rio. The silence was almost eerie as the girls walked inside and called out for Diva.

She appeared at the bottom of the staircase that led to the DJ booth, dressed down in a pair of slacks and a scoop-neck T-shirt. "So? Tell me."

"We just came from a meeting with Chico," Theresa blurted out.

"Yes?" Diva said breathlessly. "And?"

Jo shrugged. "Well, according to Chico, we're a go."

"Great!" Diva smiled, but she made a quick watch-what-you-say gesture with her hands. Naturally. Now that the business transaction was switching into high gear, they had to assume that almost any place could be wiretapped.

"We'll be meeting our . . . benefactor . . . very soon," Jo said to Diva. "And we can conduct our . . . uh, stuff."

Diva's excitement was evident from the bright flush that had come to her cheeks. "This calls for a shopping trip!" she exclaimed. "I will take you all to the best shops in Rio."

Theresa wasn't usually prone to spending sprees, unless they involved gigabytes and megahertz. But hey, they were American debutantes. It would seem strange if they *didn't* go drop a load of cash on fancy shoes and Brazilian knickknacks.

"Sounds good to me," Jo said. "I think there's a dress for doing the samba with my name on it."

"I think the votes are unanimous," Caylin said. "Let's hit the shops!"

Once the girls were outside El Centro, Diva pulled them aside. "May I go with you all for the exchange?" she asked. "More than anything, I would love to see the Big Boss go down," she added fiercely.

Theresa's instinct told her to say no. But she saw from the look on Jo's face that protestation at this point would be fruitless.

"We'll see what we can do," Jo promised. "If it's at all possible, you'll be right by our sides."

Diva nodded. "Good. I would be so honored to make the stand with you. All three of you."

Theresa smiled in sisterhood, but deep inside she hoped Jo knew what she was doing.

"Greeting, O Doubtful One, we bring glad tidings." Jo was practically bursting with adrenaline as the girls greeted Uncle Sam via speakerphone.

"Do I detect progress?" Uncle Sam asked in his usual calm manner.

"Diva thinks tomorrow is the big day," Caylin told him.

As they had shopped, Diva had let all three of them in on some of the Big Boss's ways and means of doing business. Apparently having lunch with daffy old Chico was the final step a potential business associate needed to take before the deal with the Big Boss became final. It was some kind of tradition or something.

"Bravo!" Uncle Sam said. "Excellent work, Spy Girls."

"We just have one question," Jo said. "Can we bring Diva along on the sting?"

For several seconds Sam didn't respond. "I know this young woman is our informant, but we don't know whether or not she has ulterior motives. Allowing her in on the sting could prove hazardous."

"But Diva is in just as much danger as we are!" Jo insisted. "As soon as things get funky, the bad dudes are going to suspect that she had something to do with the setup."

"Good point, Jo." There was another pause. "On second thought . . . maybe bringing your friend Diva along is a good idea," Uncle Sam said slowly. "Her intimate knowledge of the Big Boss and his underlings could prove helpful if the situation gets sticky."

"And if it turns out that she's working for the other side, we can always use her as a human shield," Theresa added.

"Come on, T., don't question Diva," Jo said, sounding like a broken record. "She's totally on the up-and-up."

"Quiet down," Uncle Sam ordered. "Spy Girls, it's time to get serious. Now, here's the plan. . . ."

"Time to switch to decaf," Jo muttered to herself the next morning. She had been up since six o'clock, and her hands were shaking—either from anticipation or the three cups of coffee she had downed while reading a daily newspaper.

She had eaten breakfast. She had updated herself on current events. She had showered and dressed in one of her supreme debutante outfits, a fresh little number courtesy of Dolce & Gabbana and, oh yes, The Tower. Still there was no word from the Big Boss. Jo didn't think she could wait much longer. Her nerves were *seriously* on the verge.

Jo heard the whir of a car engine and the slam of a door before she heard the knock at the door. Ta da! This was the moment she had been waiting for—the moment they had *all* been waiting for. As Jo walked toward the front door, she marveled at the fact that Caylin and Theresa were still asleep. For her, last night had been like Christmas Eve. Hopefully the emissary she was about to greet at the door was going to bring her the best present ever. A date with the Big Boss.

As Jo opened the door, her spirits rose even higher. The man had sent Armand, a sure sign that something major was about to go down. "Good morning, Armand."

Thank goodness she had taken the time to do up her face. If there was anyone who appreciated a pretty girl, it was Armand.

"Jacinta, it is lovely to see you again."

"Likewise." Man, when would the chitchat end? She was veritably *drowning* in polite small talk. But she had to be patient.

"I am happy to inform you that it is time to make the exchange," Armand stated formally. "There will be a car here to pick you up at five o'clock this evening." He paused. "As long as that is convenient for you ladies, of course."

Jo gave him one of her most dazzling smiles. "Well . . . we *are* expecting a shipment of new furniture this afternoon. But I'm sure we can arrange to be free by five o'clock."

"Wonderful. It's a date." Armand looked as if he would like to start the date—a *real* date—right that minute. He was looking at Jo as if she were a piece of pie on a dessert plate. "Your investment . . . is in American dollars, no?"

Jo nodded in understanding. Diva had already informed her that drug business was conducted with powerful American cash whenever possible. Speaking of which . . .

"Armand, may we bring Diva with us?" Jo asked sweetly. "She's been so instrumental in our business venture that we'd like to have her along for the celebration that will follow the . . . exchange."

Armand gave her a knowing smile. "Why, Jacinta, but of course. Diva is always welcome during business dealings." He paused. "She's practically one of the family."

Huh. Getting the okay to bring Diva in on the exchange had been easy. A more suspicious person—such as Theresa—might have even said that getting permission had been *too* easy. But Jo *wasn't* suspicious, not where Diva was concerned.

"Then we'll see you at five," Jo said.

She counted backward from ten to keep herself somewhere near a state of calm as she waited for Armand to get into his BMW convertible and peel out of the driveway. As soon as the BMW disappeared down the street, Jo raced to the speakerphone.

She pressed the button that automatically dialed Uncle Sam's number and waited breathlessly for him to come on the line.

"Speak to me," Uncle Sam greeted after only one ring.

"We're on!" Jo yelled. "Deploy the money, deploy the troops." She was torn between jumping for joy and shaking with fright. "Your Spy Girls are going into battle at precisely five o'clock this afternoon."

"Stand by," Uncle Sam ordered her. "The Tower is on its way."

Jo hung up the phone and collapsed on the sofa. Finally. The day she had been unconsciously anticipating for four years had arrived. At last Jo was going to claim justice for Judge Carreras. The man who actually pulled the trigger might remain free for the rest of his life, but thanks to Jo, a man just as bad was about to spend the rest of his life in lockdown.

Who ever said that revenge wasn't sweet?

By three o'clock in the afternoon Caylin had logged a good two hours in the window seat at the front of the mansion. The girls had paced nervously around the house all morning and afternoon, waiting, waiting, waiting for something to *happen*.

Out of nowhere, a huge furniture truck pulled into the driveway. "Hark!" Caylin screamed to the Spy Girls.

"Who goes there?" Theresa yelled back. She

and Jo were now sprinting from the kitchen to the front of the house.

"Our furniture has arrived," Caylin announced excitedly. "And it looks like there's a lot of it."

"Yee haw!" Jo yelled. "It's about time." She paused. "I guess debutantes don't say 'yee haw,' huh?"

"Who cares?" Caylin shouted. "The *furniture* is here. Finally!"

The girls rushed to the door and threw it open. "Welcome!" Theresa called. "The ergonomically correct desk chair goes in my room—right next to my laptop."

A very tall, very familiar dark-haired woman stepped out of the cab of the truck. "Very funny, Theresa. I know that you actually ordered the king-sized water bed."

"Danielle!" The cry was delivered in chorus. Their guardian angel was dressed in navy blue coveralls and a baseball cap. She was definitely the prettiest furniture deliveryman that Caylin had ever seen.

Danielle Hall was a senior Tower agent who had been assigned to help the Spy Girls through the toughest parts of some of their missions. She was always just a phone call away, and Danielle's advice and support had been oh-so-valuable during the past few months. She also had the habit of showing up at precisely the moment when she was needed most—like now.

Danielle turned back toward the huge furniture truck. "Back her up to the door, Bernie!" she yelled.

The driver waved, then maneuvered the truck so that its back was as close to the front door of the mansion as possible. Caylin watched the proceedings, fascinated. This was The Tower at its most spy-licious.

Danielle handed Caylin the key to the back of the truck. "Will you do the honors, Miss Corinne?" she asked with a wink.

"But of course." Caylin jogged to the back of the truck, inserted the key in its lock, and heaved the heavy metal door upward.

Instantly dozens of agents poured from the back of the truck into the front hall of the mansion. Many were obviously Tower agents, but others were Brazilian, shouting instructions at one another in rapid-fire Portuguese.

"Wow!" Jo exclaimed. "The commandos have arrived!"

As suddenly as it had come, the truck pulled away and disappeared down the street. Instead of furniture the Spy Girls had received a shipment of highly trained agents, a battery of high-tech surveillance equipment, and a metal briefcase stuffed with unmarked hundred-dollar bills. Yeow . . . this really was the major leagues.

"Danielle, we had no idea you were coming to save the day," Theresa exclaimed. "We would have prepared a special fairy godmother snack."

Danielle laughed. "You girls are the ones who have to save the day. I'm just here for moral support."

"Do we really need this many agents?" Caylin asked. She felt as if she were in a war bunker.

Danielle nodded. "We need extra men—and women—because of the international status of your mission. It's imperative that we have all safety, not to mention legal, potholes covered."

"I think we could supply electricity to a small nation with the amount of stuff these guys are hauling around," Jo commented. "I mean, really, who needs a laptop computer the size of a credit card?"

"I do!" Theresa yelled enthusiastically. "That way I could do my hacking even if I were locked into a small dark box."

"If you're locked in a small dark box, there's going to be a lot more to worry about than checking your e-mail," Caylin said.

Jo walked over to a gadget-filled trunk and

peered inside. "Is any of this supercool spy paraphernalia for us?"

A tall, good-looking American Tower agent stepped up to the trunk. "We've got more toys than Santa at Christmastime," he informed her.

Hmmm. Caylin had been digging the dudes in Rio, but there was nothing like an American guy who looked like he had stepped off the cover of *Surfing Magazine* to get the blood flowing.

Each of the Spy Girls reached into the trunk and pulled out a new spy gadget. Theresa got a stun gun that from all outward appearances was a lipstick. Jo acquired a variation of the mascara cam—this camera was fitted into a breath mint.

"Just make sure you don't swallow," the cute Tower dude advised.

"What's this?" Caylin asked, staring at what looked like an ordinary everyday ballpoint pen.

"That's a direct link to The Tower," Cute Agent explained. "If you click the pen, an alarm will sound at The Tower headquarters in the United States. Once Uncle Sam hears that alarm, he'll place a person-to-person call to none other than the president of the US of A."

Yikes. Caylin hoped she never had occasion to use the pen. She had no desire to create any kind of havoc in the White House.

"Listen up, Spy Chicks," Danielle called. "It's wire time."

The girls had been through this routine several times before. Each Spy Girl lifted her arms and allowed a totally hot Tower agent to attach a tiny wire to her torso. They all knew the importance of the wires.

Inside the meeting with the Big Boss, the girls would be on their own. The agents would be waiting outside, ready to burst in and make their arrests once the girls had sufficient evidence on tape. They could also raid the place in the unfortunate event that the whole deal went sour and the Spy Girls were in imminent danger. If the agents lost their ability to hear what was going on inside the meeting—for whatever reason—the girls could kiss the mission good-bye.

"Do we know the meeting place?" Danielle asked, consulting her notes.

Caylin shook her head. "We don't even know the Big Boss's name, much less where the handover is going to occur."

Danielle nodded. "That's too bad . . . but we'll manage. The second you get into that car, we'll be on your tail—from a distance, of course."

"What happens if the driver figures out somebody is following us?" Theresa asked anxiously.

Danielle raised her eyebrows. "He won't."

Caylin shivered with anticipation. The sting was elaborate, but the agents seemed to know what they were doing. As long as she and her *compadres* upheld their end of the operation, all would go smoothly. She hoped.

Danielle glanced at her watch. "It's four forty-five," she announced. "Show time."

Dingdong. The doorbell rang at exactly five o'clock. Theresa touched the wire taped to her body one last time, her heart beating wildly.

"We'll be fine," Caylin said.

"We'll be better than fine," Jo corrected her. "We're going to kick some major drug-lord butt."

Theresa nodded. They had been in tight situations before—and they had, indeed, kicked butt. "We look great, we feel great, and we have a metal briefcase filled with hundred-dollar bills."

Jo laughed. "I couldn't have said it better myself." She paused. "So why do I feel like I'm going to barf?"

Unfortunately for all of them, there was no time to run to the nearest bathroom and throw up. As Danielle had put it so succinctly, this was show time. Theresa opened the door and found herself face-to-face with the charming Armand.

"Good afternoon, lovely ladies. It is a glorious evening for business, no?" Armand walked into the foyer and bowed slightly from the waist.

"We can hardly wait," Caylin agreed. Only her fellow Spy Girls would have been able to detect the small tremor in her voice as she spoke.

"Shall we go?" Jo asked. Caylin noticed that her eyes had drifted toward the staircase.

"By all means," Armand replied. He stepped aside to allow the three of them to leave the house in front of him. There were those manners again.

Caylin and Jo stepped outside and headed toward the limo parked in the driveway. As Theresa followed, Armand lightly touched her arm.

"Where is your new furniture, Trixie?" Armand inquired, looking into the living room.

Theresa thought fast. Very fast. "Oh, it's all upstairs." Well, it wasn't *exactly* a lie—all their human, technological, and otherwise resources had taken a powder to the second floor fifteen minutes previous. "We got new . . . um, bedroom sets."

"Maybe later you'll show me, yes?"

Theresa smiled and lowered her eyes de-
murely. Yeah, right, she thought. Maybe later he
would be in *jail.*

As she walked out the front door, Theresa
turned and glanced once more into the house.
Danielle's head popped out from behind the
door that led to the kitchen, and she flashed a
big thumbs-up. Theresa smiled, taking a deep
breath. This was it. They would either come
back to the mansion victorious—or they
wouldn't come back at all.

"ello, friends. It's a glorious evening for doing business, no?" Diva greeted the Spy Girls as she slid into the back of the limousine.

Jo had a perverse urge to giggle. Armand had used almost exactly the same words less than twenty minutes ago. If he only knew how different they sounded coming from Diva's mouth . . .

"Hi, Diva," Theresa greeted her warmly. Thank goodness. At last Theresa seemed to have let go of her paranoid suspicion of their greatest ally.

The driver drove out of El Centro's parking lot and pulled into traffic. Wow—rush hour was the same all over the world, apparently. Jo knew that it was beyond important that her demeanor remain calm, cool, and collected, but the international agent in her worried about The Tower's ability to trail the limo in this much traffic. Why couldn't the summit meeting have been set for a time that coincided with afternoon siesta?

As Jo stared—surreptitiously, she hoped—out the back window, Diva reached over and squeezed her arm. "We're in this together, Jacinta," she whispered softly.

Jo felt herself relax. Diva was a kindred spirit. She would look out for the girls, no matter what went down.

Up in the front, Armand was humming a salsa tune. "How are you doing, lovely ladies?" He turned and stared at them.

"Peachy," Theresa squeaked. "This is the *best*."

Good thing Armand didn't know Theresa better than he did. The fact that she had uttered a word like *peachy* was a clear indication that she was way past nervous.

Armand snorted. "The American girls are a little unsure, yes?" He winked at Diva. "They are new at this game."

"Don't let our youth fool you," Caylin told him coolly. "We've been around more than a few blocks in our time."

"*Rrrow* . . . feisty." Armand growled flirtatiously in Caylin's direction. "Maybe yours is the bedroom set I would like to see later tonight, ah?"

Jo resisted the urge to roll her eyes. Armand,

gorgeous or not, was one aspect of this mission she wouldn't miss. His blatant come-ons bordered on nauseating. Instead of the eye roll, she let her lids droop. Shutting out the rest of the world was essential at this particular moment. Otherwise all sorts of haunting images might mess with her focus.

"I'm here, Jacinta." Again Diva squeezed her arm.

Jo grinned. They had been right to bring Diva along. She was sure of that now. Their new friend was an integral part of this crime organization, and she knew better than any of them what was up. As long as Diva stayed cool, nothing could *possibly* go wrong. . . .

"And I thought *we* had nice digs," Caylin commented as the girls climbed out of the limo thirty minutes later. "This place isn't a home . . . it's a city."

They had arrived at one of the most ginormous estates Caylin had ever seen. The front lawn—if the term *lawn* applied to an expanse of grass that large—was perfectly manicured. Several fountains dotted the landscape, and there were no less than three incredibly expensive sports cars parked in the driveway-slash-road.

Armand brushed past the girls and opened

the front door without knocking. "Honey, I'm home!" He smiled at Caylin. "That's a little bit of American humor for you, yes?"

Caylin didn't bother to respond. Instead she gaped at the massive, opulent foyer into which Armand had led them. Yowza! Floor-to-ceiling white marble and a chandelier big enough for all three Spy Girls *and* Uncle Sam to swing from. This was definitely the Big Boss's den. The place shouted *dinero*.

"Ah, ladies, how lovely is it to see you again." Chico doddered in from an unidentified room off the front hall.

He was looking significantly more suave than he had during their lunch meeting. Today he was wearing an Armani suit, and a shiny diamond ring glittered on his right pinky finger.

Chico's eyes lit up when he saw Diva. "Ah, my girl . . ." He clasped her arms and kissed her on each cheek. "We have been expecting you."

Diva returned the kisses. "So, where is the meeting to take place?" she asked Chico.

Good for her. Just like a real Spy Girl, Diva had gotten straight to the point. Caylin gave her a silent cheer. If they didn't get this meeting going pronto, Caylin wasn't going to be able to keep the butterflies in her stomach from flying free.

"This way." Chico turned and headed down a long, narrow hallway. The girls fell into line, following his footsteps in nervous silence.

There was a veritable gang of gangsters waiting for the debutante party in a large den. Caylin had rarely seen more men in expensive suits in one place at one time. All of the hotties from their night at La Americana were present, as well as several beefy bodyguard types who looked as if they had been recruited from the World Wrestling Federation. Alas, there was still no sign of the Big Boss. Hopefully he was nearby.

Caylin sized up the situation. There were two doors. One was behind Chico, who had retreated to the back of the room immediately. The other was behind Jo, who still hovered in front of the door the girls had come through. Meanwhile the metal briefcase in Theresa's left hand was clearly the center of attention. Every man in the room was staring lustfully at that case full o' cash.

Chico cleared his throat—apparently to distract everyone's attention from the half a million dollars at the end of Theresa's arm. "Now . . . we do business."

Ready. Set. Run. The sting was on.

Jo had looked forward to a day like this one ever since the day her father's killer had been set free. But now that the moment had arrived, she felt almost paralyzed with fear.

Any one of these men could take out a gun at a moment's notice and blow her brains out. Literally. Then again, at a moment's notice the American and Brazilian agents could charge into the room and take each and every one of these men into custody. At least, they could charge in here as long as they had managed to tail the trio and the wires were operational. Otherwise backup was more or less powerless to come in and do its thing when the time was right. Otherwise the three of them were totally and completely on their own—and poor Diva would be added to the endangered species list.

"I believe you have five hundred thousand dollars for us?" Chico asked Theresa.

The gulp was almost audible. "And I believe that you're willing to offer us a guaranteed twenty-five percent profit on our investment?"

Diva had informed the girls that twenty-five percent was a standard return on an investment in the drug trade. Thank goodness Theresa had maintained the presence of mind to spell it out for the always important wiretap. At the moment Jo wasn't sure she could remember her own vital statistics.

"Yes, of course, Trixie. That *is* the industry

standard." Hmmm. Apparently Chico's English was better than he had let on.

Theresa held out the briefcase. "It's all there, Chico."

Jorge stepped forward, took the briefcase, then handed it to Chico. "Heavy," Chico commented. He laid the case on a mahogany table and flipped open the lid. Every person in the room stared at the green-and-white bills.

Chico smiled. "Beautiful!" He reached into the briefcase and laid his hands on the money. "There is nothing like the smell of new American dollars to put spring in an old man's step." He shut the case and snapped the lock shut.

Jo's entire body tensed as Chico walked toward the door at the back of the room. He turned down the dimmer on the overhead light switch, then opened the door. "It's ready."

A moment later a man stepped through the door. His face remained in shadow, but it was clear to Jo that this was the long-awaited Big Boss.

"The young ladies have officially invested in our business," Chico informed the boss. "The money is all yours." Chico picked up the briefcase and held it out to his superior.

"Wonderful." The Big Boss accepted the money, then stepped out of the shadows.

Jo stared at the face of the man the Spy Girls were about to bring down. As she absorbed the details of his features, the world started to shift around her. No! It wasn't possible!

"I—" Jo looked into the man's coal black eyes . . . and recognized him. In a flash, she saw that he recognized her as well.

"What is it?" Theresa asked.

Jo blinked rapidly as her father's murder flashed through her mind in a series of rapid, surreal images. Yes, she knew this man. She had seen him in her nightmares for years.

"You—you killed my father!" Jo screamed.

Theresa felt as if time had stopped as she watched Jo scream at the Big Boss. "We need backup *now!*" she yelled into her wiretap.

"I remember! I saw you!" Jo was yelling at the Big Boss, but her words were broken with loud, hoarse sobs. Meanwhile Diva was shaking. Her face had gone deathly pale.

The Big Boss's eyes were wide and scared. He looked toward Chico. "What is this?" the man shouted.

Chico took a step backward, away from the Big Boss. "I don't know!"

Pandemonium erupted in the room as Jo continued to shout accusations at the man in front of her. Everything was happening so fast that Theresa could barely process the events. All she knew for sure was that the sting was in serious jeopardy—not to mention their lives.

"No!" The Big Boss turned from Jo and began to run toward the door at the back of the room.

"He killed my father!" Jo screamed again.

Every man in the room pulled a gun from the waistband of his suit. Armand shouted in Portuguese while Chico fixed Jo with a cold, brutal stare. Oh no. This was it. They were all going to die.

"Where are the agents?" Caylin hissed.

Suddenly the door behind Theresa burst open. Instantly dozens of agents poured into the room. "Freeze!" someone screamed.

In seconds the agents had each of the Big Boss's underlings on the floor and in hand-cuffs. But the Big Boss was escaping through the back door.

"Over there!" Theresa screamed, pointing in the direction of the Big Boss.

"What are you doing?" Diva screamed at Theresa. Her eyes were dark and wild. She looked like a desperate, trapped animal. "You've got the wrong man! That man is innocent!"

Diva clutched Theresa's arms, shaking her. "Do you hear me? He is *innocent!*"

"Get him!" Theresa ordered.

Two agents leaped over the desk and disappeared behind the door. Thirty seconds later they reappeared with the man who had killed Jo's father.

"You're going to the electric chair!" Jo shouted. "I'm going to see you *fry.*"

Jo's words seemed to be coming from some primal, previously unknown part of her soul. Theresa had never seen her friend break down like this—it was frightening.

"Jacinta, no!" Diva moaned. "He is innocent!" Diva collapsed into a chair and sobbed hysterically.

"What are you talking about?" Caylin yelled, shaking Diva's shoulders.

"*That* man is my *father!*" Diva cried. "Chico is the one you want!"

Caylin didn't know whether to cry or breathe a huge sigh of relief. The Big Boss had been taken into custody, but Jo was a basket case. Nothing seemed to make sense.

Chico was shaking his head as he studied Diva's tear-stained face. "Diva, how can you say such things? You know I commit no crime. I am a pawn in the game of your father—just like all these men."

"You liar!" Diva cried. "He's lying!"

Again Chico shook his head. "I trusted you, Diva . . . but I forget you are like your father—a cold-blooded killer."

"Explain yourself," barked the agent holding Chico by the arm.

"I have been faithful to Diva's father as his second in command for many years—on pain of death." He sighed deeply. "But that wasn't enough for this family. They wanted me put in jail so that Diva could take over at her father's right hand. It wouldn't be enough to kill me.

No, they want to put me away for their crimes. They want me to die, an old man, alone in prison."

Diva stood up and took the place beside her father. "No, *we* are the pawns. Chico has been controlling our lives for as long as I can remember."

"They no longer want this old man around," Chico commented, shrugging at one of the agents. "No respect, they have. Too much trouble I cause for them. They find me weak—senile, yes? Thank goodness I call for your help. But they find out I give information to you, and all this"—he waved his arms around the den—"this plan with you ladies, with the money, this was to punish me for telling. But now you have made me safe. And now I can be free."

Danielle put a hand on Jo's shoulder and pointed toward Diva's father, who was staring at Jo in horror. "Are you absolutely sure that's the man who killed your father?" Danielle asked.

Jo nodded. "I'll never forget his face."

"Take him away, boys," Danielle instructed the agents. "We've got our man."

"No!" Diva tried to hold on to her father, but two agents grabbed her arms and held her tightly.

## Dial "V" for Vengeance

"I love you, Diva!" her father cried as the agents pushed him toward the door. "We'll get through this!"

Diva watched as her father disappeared with the agents. She seemed to be in as bad shape as Jo. Then she turned to Caylin and grabbed her arm. "You've got to listen!" Diva cried. "They're taking the wrong man!"

Armand smiled at Theresa, Jo, and Caylin, despite the fact that he was wearing a pair of handcuffs and had a gun pointed toward his shoulder. "Thank you, ladies. Your brave actions have saved the world from suffering at the hands of that man—the cruelest man I have ever known. He thought with his business, he could control us all. Power hungry, I think you call it."

Caylin didn't know what to believe. She didn't even fully understand what was going on around her. There were a million unanswered questions. But the Spy Girls had a right to know the answers. Especially Jo. Caylin glanced at her weeping friend and felt her own eyes well up with tears. Sometimes it seemed as if there was simply too much tragedy in the world for one super-duper Spy Girl to bear.

Jo forced herself to stop crying. She had spent too many years shedding tears. Now was

117

the time for anger. Righteous, indignant rage. Slowly everything was becoming all too clear.

Diva wasn't just trying to set up Chico. She had also been setting up Jo. Diva and her father had wanted to twist the knife into Jo and her family even further than they had when they killed Judge Carreras. They had wanted to sit back and *laugh* at stupid, gullible Jo. Oh yes. Diva had known all along that Jacinta was actually Josefina Mercedes Carreras.

Jo turned to Diva, who was still standing under an antique shield. She glared at her with all the hatred and venom she could muster. "How could you?" she asked. "You knew your father killed my father. And what do you do? You *used* that against me! All that stuff about 'my father is in danger'—what a load. All you wanted to do was play on my vulnerability and win my trust. You're disgusting."

"You're wrong!" Diva cried. "I don't even know what you're talking about!"

"Yes, you do," Jo said, her voice steely. "You used my father's memory to further your own evil schemes."

"I told you, I have no idea what you're talking about, Jacinta." Diva's cheeks were ashen, and her dark eyes were rimmed with red. "I only wanted us to help each other bring down the Big Boss!"

Jo let out a sound that was somewhere between a laugh and a sob. "Help me? How does killing my dad *help* me?" Jo walked toward Diva so that the traitor could see the disgust in Jo's eyes as she listened to her speak.

"Your father killed my father, Diva. Four years ago. In Miami. He killed him right in front of me."

"Oh . . . no!" Diva brought her hands to her face. "That day . . . oh, that horrible day. . . ." She paused. "You—you're Josefina Carreras?"

Josefina Carreras. Josefina Mercedes Carreras. Jo hadn't been called "Josefina" in years. Since the day her father had been killed, woe be to anyone who dared called her anything but "Jo."

"You know I am," Jo spat. "You've known that all along. And you cried those fake, crocodile tears over the treachery of the drug trade to win my trust."

Diva's face turned from pale to even paler. Her body began to sway back and forth, and for a moment it looked as if she were going to faint. "I needed you," she muttered. "I needed your help, and—"

"Take her," Danielle said suddenly. "She belongs in custody right beside her father."

Before Diva could fall to the floor, two agents grabbed her arms and propped her up.

As they dragged her toward the door, Jo waited to feel some small measure of satisfaction. But she didn't. All she felt was the deep, aching, vast loss of her father. It was as if she had just witnessed his murder all over again.

Jo felt Theresa place an arm around her shoulders. "Let's get out of here, Jo."

"I'm going to see that they get what they deserve," Jo told Theresa.

"We all will," Caylin promised.

Jo allowed her fellow Spy Girls to wrap her in a warm embrace. Diva had betrayed her, but Theresa and Caylin would be her friends forever. After several long moments Jo pulled away, feeling a bit more like herself.

"Five minutes alone with those two," she said. "That's all I want." She knew exactly what she would do and how she would do it. . . .

Three hours later Theresa fought the urge to pull an I-told-you-so on Jo. After the threesome had returned to the mansion for a depressurization break, Danielle had driven them to the ultrasecret holding area where Tower agents were now questioning Diva and her father. Safely ensconced behind a two-way mirror, Theresa, Caylin, Jo, and Danielle were watching the interrogation from just several feet away.

"I shouldn't have trusted her," Jo muttered for the fifth time. "How could I have been so stupid?"

"We all trusted her, Jo," Caylin said soothingly. "Diva seemed like a stand-up chick."

Theresa nodded. Yes, she had held on to her suspicions regarding Diva for a long time, but the truth was that she had eventually believed in their informant as much as Jo and Caylin had.

"Listen to them," Danielle said. "They're pros."

The girls redirected their attention to the interrogation. Diva and her father were all wide eyes and innocence as they talked to The Tower agents. Danielle was right. If Theresa didn't know better, she would have felt sympathy toward the pair.

"My daughter only wanted to help our family," the Big Boss was saying. "Even if you feel that I have done wrong, please let her go. She is an innocent child."

Yet another fake tear slid down Diva's cheek. "No, Father! I am not going to let them believe these evil lies about you. We must help them learn the truth!"

The Big Boss shook his head sadly. Man, he was good. "They will believe what they want to believe, Diva."

Diva clutched her father's arm as she stared into the face of her interrogator. "You have to listen to me! *I'm* the person who brought your agents to Rio! Not Chico! Why would I have done that if my father and I were guilty of all of these horrible crimes? We're victims . . . just like Josefina."

Jo snorted. "She makes me sick—and I make me sick. It was obvious all along that Diva was this close to the Big Boss."

"You're right, Jo," Caylin said. "I mean, we should have gotten a clue way back when we found out that Diva *owned* a nightclub that was basically a front for drug trafficking."

"Or when the Big Boss's emissaries were so cool about Diva coming with us for the money exchange," Theresa commented.

"The important thing is that you three came through in the end," Danielle said firmly. "Jo, you recognized Diva's father when the time was right. And now they're both going to spend a long time behind bars."

Danielle had a good point. Even though Diva turned out to be a bad guy, she *had* led them to her father. Without her involvement, the Spy Girls never would have gotten to him.

"I can't believe she took us for such fools," Jo said. "Did she really think I wouldn't recognize her dad?"

Theresa shrugged. "Criminals can be arrogant. Look at them—even now they're trying to maintain their innocent sob story."

"I'm just glad that the man who killed your father is finally going to be locked away forever," Caylin said.

"And Diva can rot in jail right along beside him," Jo added. "She's as bad as he is. . . . I don't think I've ever felt so betrayed by another human being."

"The agents are finishing up the interview," Danielle interrupted. "Any moment, father and daughter are going to be taken to the cells where they belong."

Once again Theresa turned her attention back to the room in front of them. Diva and the Big Boss were now on their feet, agents at their sides. Slowly they began to walk from the room.

"Wait!" Diva yelled suddenly. She broke free from the agents' grasp and lunged toward the mirror. Her eyes were wild as she pressed her face against the two-way glass.

"The gun!" Diva yelled. "Remember the gun!" Before she could say another word, the agents regained their control of her and led both suspects from the room.

"What did she mean by that?" Theresa wondered aloud. "Remember the gun. . . ."

Caylin shrugged. "Who knows? Maybe it's some kind of weird organized-crime slogan."

"I don't know, and I don't care," Jo said. "But at least this mission is over with."

Theresa nodded. The mission was over. Unfortunately, not one of them was in the mood to celebrate.

heck out all the amazing clothes we acquired during this mission," Caylin said to Jo. "I can't wait to wear these duds back in the States."

"Maybe I'll change my image," Theresa added brightly. "I'll turn in my khakis for a dressy evening gown."

Jo shrugged. "You can have my stuff. I don't feel like dealing with the whole packing thing."

Caylin exchanged a glance with Theresa. This was *not* the Jo they knew and loved. But nothing they said or did seemed to be helping to bring her out of her funk. And they had said and done just about *everything*. The girls had come straight back to HQ after the interrogation, and they had spent the last hour trying to cheer up Jo while they got ready to head back to the United States. Unfortunately, nothing was working.

"Mind if I come in?" Danielle was standing

at the door of Jo's room, looking more maternal than usual.

"Please do." Caylin hoped Danielle had the magic words because she and Theresa were crashing and burning over and over again.

Danielle sat down on the queen-sized bed and looked thoughtfully at Jo for a few moments. "I know this mission has been tough for you, Jo. But you should be extremely proud of yourself. Not many daughters of murder victims are able to be responsible for the ultimate conviction of their loved one's killer."

Jo sighed. "I know, Danielle. . . . I'm just so drained. After reliving all of those awful memories, I feel totally and completely tapped out—like I could get into bed and sleep for a hundred years."

"All of you girls deserve a—" Danielle's statement was cut off by the sound of someone knocking at the door.

"Did anyone order a pizza?" Caylin asked, making yet one more attempt at a lame joke. When no one responded, she shrugged. "I'll get it."

"We'll all get it," Danielle said, heaving herself off the bed. "You never know who might be paying us a not so friendly visit."

The group trooped downstairs, where Caylin opened the front door warily. Standing on the front step was none other than Chico—and he was holding one of the biggest vases of flowers Caylin had ever laid eyes on.

"I have come to express gratitude to you wonderful girls," Chico said. He bowed deeply. "Thank to your courage, I can live like a normal person without fearing that horrible, horrible man."

"You have been totally exonerated, then?" Danielle asked.

Chico nodded. "The agents are now aware that it was I who make communication to The Tower. Diva, she discovered my betrayal and take control herself. But I was meant to be the one you meet in Rio."

"I'm glad your world is safe again," Jo said. For the first time since she recognized Diva's father, Jo sounded like her old self. Thank goodness.

Again Chico bowed. "You girls are my heroes."

Jo stepped forward and embraced Chico. "You know, you remind me of my grandfather. He died when I was young, but he looked a lot like you."

"I am please to hear you said that," Chico responded.

Jo laughed. "I am please to have said it."

Chico grinned, his blue eyes twinkling. "How long will your visit to Brazil be?"

"We're leaving in the morning," Theresa answered. "We've got to get out of here to make way for the new occupants of this place . . . and I'm sure we've got some kind of duty calling for us back in America."

Chico frowned. "But this is nonsense! You must rest. And I would like to help you—in my own home."

"What do you mean?" Caylin asked. Her ears had perked up at the word *rest*. Jo wasn't the only one who was wiped out.

"My house is not large . . . but I would love to offer to you for vacation. In my appreciation, I can give you my home. And I have enough money save to offer you girls your every wish. If only for this short time."

"That does sound tempting," Jo admitted.

"Please, be my guest. My grandson will love me all forever. He comes to visit tomorrow, and he would love these beautiful girls. . . . He is very handsome."

This scenario was sounding better and better. Great R and R, cute grandson, lazy afternoon by the pool . . . Caylin turned to Danielle.

"What do you say?" she asked.

Danielle smiled. "I *do* think you girls deserve a little time out—but only for a few days."

Jo grinned at Chico. Her first *real* smile all day. "You're on, Chico. For the next few days we're going to let our troubles melt in the sun."

Caylin laughed aloud. This was exactly what they needed. Peace, quiet, and a chance for holiday romance. Before long, everything in the world o' the Spy Girls would be back to normal.

"Have I at all mentioned in the last five minutes just how totally awesome Danielle is?" Theresa asked the next afternoon. "I don't think I've been this relaxed since before Spy Girl training camp."

She picked up a bottle of SPF 30 to apply yet another layer of sunscreen to her face. The Brazilian sun wasn't something to mess around with, no matter how amazing it felt washing over Theresa's body.

Caylin flipped a page of a magazine that was Brazil's answer to *Teen People* and glanced at Theresa over the top of her huge mirrored sunglasses. "If we had known what a way Danielle has with Uncle Sam, we could have begged her to scam us vacation time from day one."

"We didn't *need* the vacation on day one," Jo commented. "Now we do."

"Good point," Theresa said.

After Chico's visit the night before, Danielle had dialed up Uncle Sam and managed to wheedle a few Spy Girl vacation days from their demanding—if lovable—boss. Go, Danielle!

The trio had spent the rest of the evening packing and waxing nostalgic about the details of their previous missions. By the time they had arrived at Chico's this morning, Jo had been at least semirestored to her old self—which was evidenced by her promise to give yet one more go at trying to teach Theresa the samba.

Theresa had closed her eyes against the bright sun, but now she felt a presence beside her chair. She opened her eyes and found herself staring at Chico—and the promised grandson. Yes, indeed, said grandson lived up to grandpa's handsome description. Even a self-confessed geek like Theresa could appreciate green eyes, jet black hair, and well-sculpted chest muscles.

"Why, *hello,*" Caylin greeted them, beating both of her fellow Spy Girls to the proverbial punch. "We have been *so* looking forward to making your acquaintance."

"Girls, this is my grandson, Pedro. He told me by the window that he never sees girls this beautiful."

"Pull up a lounge chair, Pedro," Jo said, stretching her legs in a way that practically made the grandson's oh-so-*very*-green eyes pop out of his head.

Chico laughed. "Good. You are all friends now, yes?"

"Yes," Theresa said quickly. She had to say *something* before one of the other SGs cornered their latest prey.

"I must go now," Chico said. "The other men and I . . . we have what you call to complete unfinished business at the boss's home."

Theresa shuddered. She wouldn't set foot in that vast place again for a million dollars. She much preferred Chico's pad, which was just large enough, comfortable, and homey—not to mention loaded with yummy food and hottie grandsons.

"Good luck!" Caylin called to Chico, obviously eager to usher Chico past the pool and out to his car so that she could focus on reeling in Pedro.

Theresa giggled. At last things really were back to the way they should be. Ah . . . paradise.

Jo smiled and nodded and flirted as Theresa and Caylin anxiously studied her face for signs that she was over the trauma of the last few days. But she wasn't over it. Not even close.

In her mind, Jo replayed almost every word of every interaction she'd had with Diva over the past several days. How could Jo have been so naive as to trust someone with such a treacherous heart? It seemed impossible. And as for Diva—could even Meryl Streep have faked the kind of emotion that Jo had read on her face and in her eyes?

"Jo! Earth to Jo!" Caylin was snapping her fingers in front of Jo's dark sunglasses.

"Sorry . . . I guess I sort of spaced out."

"Would you like a limeade? Or fresh orange juice? Pedro is waiting for your answer."

Jo glanced at Pedro. Mmmm. He really was a cutie. At any other time, she would have been turning on the flirt. "Oh . . . limeade, I guess."

As she watched Pedro retreat into the house, Jo allowed her thoughts to wander back to Diva. Their so-called friend had been so adamant about her father's innocence and her desire to help the Spy Girls.

Was it possible . . . ? No. Definitely not. All of the evidence established Diva's guilt beyond a shadow of a doubt. But then again, Jo knew that sometimes evidence had a tendency to fall through the cracks.

*Remember the gun.* Diva's words echoed over and over in Jo's mind. The gun. What gun? Where? Clearly Diva had thought that the image of a gun would resonate with the Spy Girls. There had to be something there. . . .

Suddenly Jo sat up straight in her lounge

chair. She had a crazy, irrational, nutso idea. But it was an idea nonetheless.

"Hey, Trixie, do you have your laptop handy?" she asked Theresa.

"Sure. It's upstairs in my room. I never leave home without it. Why?"

Jo jumped off the lounger and grabbed her enormous beach towel. "I want to go upstairs to surf the Internet. There are some old *Miami Herald* articles I have to read."

"What articles?" Theresa asked.

"The ones about my father," Jo said gravely. "I think it's time we do a little more investigation—Spy Girl style."

re you sure you want to be doing this, Jo?" Theresa had turned on her laptop and logged onto the Internet, but she had made it clear that she wasn't convinced Jo had all her wits about her.

"Positive." Jo was hovering behind Theresa's shoulder, staring at the screen.

"You haven't had to dwell on the details of your dad's murder for a long time," Caylin pointed out. "Going through all of those articles is going to bring back a lot of awful memories."

"I appreciate your concern—I really do," Jo insisted. "But I live with the fact that my father was killed every day . . . and if there's even the slightest chance that I'm missing some piece of the puzzle, I want to find out."

"Okay . . ." Theresa clicked onto an Internet search engine, then typed in instructions for the engine to browse archived issues of *The Miami Herald.*

Jo focused on the whir of the computer as she tried to mentally prepare herself for this journey into the past. Shortly after that joke of a trial for Diva's father, Jo had forced herself to shut out the specifics of the case. Pondering the evidence had been driving Jo crazy—so crazy that she'd had to forget the majority of the evidence just to put her life back together and find the strength to move on. Well, she had moved on. But as the saying went, the past had always been close behind. And now Jo was about to turn around and face it.

"Here you are, Jo," Theresa said, interrupting her thoughts. "I managed to narrow the search to *Miami Herald* articles specifically relating to the trial. Just click the mouse . . . and you can read as much—or as little—as you want to."

Theresa slid out of the desk chair, and Jo took her place. She clicked onto the first article: "Miami Judge Shot and Killed." And there it was, in black and white. The story of her father's murder, complete with a photograph of a blood-spattered Jo crying at the scene of the crime.

"Do you remember anything about the case?" Theresa asked quietly. "It might help to refresh your memory before you go any further with this."

Jo bit her lip. "There was something about a murder weapon—or a lack of a murder weapon. I remember that being mentioned over and over again on the local TV news."

"We'll find out soon enough," Caylin said. "If they talked about the murder weapon on the news, they'll definitely mention it in these articles."

Jo clicked quickly through several more articles, searching for one that discussed the details of the trial at length. Finally she found a feature that had been written shortly after Diva's father had been freed. Yes. This was exactly what she had been looking for. She perused the article while Caylin and Theresa read over her shoulders.

"Now I remember," Jo said slowly. "According to the police lab, my dad was killed with a bullet fired from a rare gun. There were only five of them made."

"Wow . . . that's a pretty strong piece of evidence," Theresa said. "I can't believe they couldn't convict the guy with that."

Jo shook her head. "That's the thing. Four of the guns were being kept in museums or stored away safely in known private collections at the time. There was no way any of them could have been used in the shooting."

"And the fifth gun was never located," Theresa

read aloud. "Whoa . . . that's pretty creepy."

"The gun Diva's father had in possession at the time he was arrested was a different make," Caylin continued. "And lab reports proved that the second gun wasn't fired that day."

"Which is why that evidence was thrown out of court and the guy was ultimately acquitted," Jo concluded. "Have you ever heard such a suspicious story?"

"No kidding," Theresa said. "It sounds like *somebody* paid off a crooked judge or a dirty crime lab official."

"Exactly." Jo stared at the article, paragraph after paragraph explaining away the guilt of her father's murderer. "At the time, that's exactly what I thought. Which is why I had to make myself forget all of this."

"What do you think now?" Caylin asked hesitantly.

Jo sighed. "I don't know . . . but I think that fifth gun might prove to be the key to learning the truth." She paused. "I *have* to know where that fifth gun is. Period. And something tells me it's somewhere in Rio."

Caylin glanced at Theresa. She knew that her friend was thinking exactly what Caylin herself was. Jo's interest in the fifth gun spelled trouble.

"Jo, your dad's killer is finally in jail. Don't you think it's time to let it go?"

"Maybe. But I can't." Jo left her post in front of the computer screen and flopped onto the large bed. "I want to know the truth."

"We understand where you're coming from," Theresa said, perching beside Jo. "But the mission is over. It's time for all of us to relax. We need to regain our strength so that we'll be properly geared up for the next mission—whatever it is."

"You guys can go ahead and relax all you want," Jo said firmly. "I want to find that gun."

"This is crazy, Jo. You know Uncle Sam wouldn't approve of us poking our noses into Tower business at this stage of the game." Caylin had raised her voice to emphasize her point.

Jo remained silent, staring into space with an eerie expression on her face. Caylin was about to try a different tack to get Jo's mind off the fifth gun—but she swallowed her words when there was a knock on Theresa's bedroom door.

"Yes?" Theresa asked, opening the door.

"Mr. Chico is home," Maria, Chico's house-keeper announced. Then she said something in Portuguese that Caylin couldn't follow whatsoever.

"She says dinner is in fifteen minutes," Jo

translated. At last she seemed to have come out of her trance.

After Maria was gone, Theresa slung her arm around Jo's shoulders. "Will you promise us to let this go?" she asked.

Jo nodded. "I will. At least for now."

Caylin breathed a huge sigh of relief. Jo was a reasonable enough chick. Once she'd had a chance to sleep on her decision to find that gun, she would realize that she was making a big mistake . . . hopefully.

Jo had continued to ponder the missing fifth gun throughout the first and second courses of dinner. But she was careful to mask her thoughts behind a bright, interested exterior. Above all else, she didn't want Theresa and Caylin to know just how serious she was about her quest for the truth—whatever it was.

"Brazil really is a gorgeous country," Theresa was saying to Chico. "Someday I would love to come back and spend more time here."

"You will always be welcome as our guest, eh, Pedro?" Chico said, winking at his grandson.

"Of course," Pedro returned. "All of the girls are welcome."

Jo was handing her plate to a white-jacketed male servant as the telephone rang somewhere deep within the house. Instantly Jo tensed.

## Dial "V" for Vengeance

A moment later Maria appeared at the entrance of the dining room. "Excuse me, sir, the *telefone* is for Miss Jacinta." Although The Tower had been convinced that Chico was on the up-and-up, the girls had continued to use their aliases. By now, everyone was used to them.

"Who is it?" Caylin asked, her voice laden with suspicion.

"She say Danielle," Maria answered in her somewhat broken English.

Jo pushed her chair out from the table. "I'll just be a second," she told Chico. "Danielle probably just wants to talk about travel plans or something."

Jo followed Maria farther into the house and picked up the receiver of a phone in a small den off the living room. "Hello?"

"Josefina, it is me."

She had known, somewhere deep inside her, that Danielle wouldn't be on the other end of the line. And Jo had been right. She recognized the traitor's voice immediately.

It was Diva. Jo whispered, "Where are you? Why are you calling me?"

"I cannot talk now. But I need to speak with you as soon as possible. It's about the gun."

The gun. Diva had implored her to remember the gun. But Jo wasn't a fool. Diva wasn't going to win back her trust by mentioning a gun that turned up missing four years ago.

"Why should I talk to you?" Jo asked. "And last I heard, you were rotting in jail."

"Meet me behind the club at nine o'clock tonight." Diva's whispered voice was urgent, pleading. "Please. For the sake of my father . . . and the memory of yours."

The phone went dead, and Jo replaced the receiver in its cradle. She had known from the instant she heard Diva's voice on the other end of the line that she would listen to what the girl had to say. Something was driving Jo forward, and she owed it to herself—and her father—to find out what that something was.

Jo reentered the dining room and took her place at the table as if she didn't have a care in the world. But her appetite was gone, and her mind was already several miles away—several miles away and behind El Centro, to be exact.

"What did Danielle want?" Caylin asked.

Jo shrugged. "She left her favorite bikini at the other house. I told her I'd swing by and pick it up after dinner."

"We'll come along and keep you company," Theresa offered. "I haven't had a ride in the Alfa Romeo all day—a new record for us."

Uh. That wasn't going to work. Not at all. Theresa and Caylin would never approve of Jo going to talk to Diva without clearing the rendezvous with The Tower first. And Jo's gut instinct told her that Uncle Sam wasn't going to okay any clandestine meetings with the Big Boss's daughter.

"I'd like to hang here," Caylin said. "Pedro and I were going to take a dip in the pool."

Jo breathed an inner sigh of relief. Getting rid of her ever present comrades was going to be easier than she had expected. "If you guys don't mind, I think I'll go on my own. I think a little solo jaunt would help me clear out my head once and for all."

Theresa nodded understandingly. "I see what you mean." She leaned close to Jo. "And I'll keep an eye on Caylin—so she doesn't make too much headway in your absence," she added in a whisper.

Jo leaned back in her chair and surveyed the crowded table. Everyone continued to eat and drink as if some possibly momentous event wasn't about to take place. But Jo knew differently. She knew that tonight might change everything.

"Hello, Diva." Jo had fled Chico's home without a hitch and sped all the way to El Centro. Diva had been waiting in the shadows behind the club, just as she had promised.

143

"Josefina, you must listen to me. My father is innocent."

"How did you get out of jail?" Jo asked. "Did you escape?" Even in the darkness, Jo could see that Diva looked terrible. Her face was pale, and her eyes were swollen from crying. She even thought that more of Diva's hair had turned white.

"No, the agents let me go . . . at least for now. They believe that I only did what I did because my father forced me to."

"Is that true?" Jo asked.

Diva shook her head. "No. I did what I did because of Chico. He is the one who has held all of us hostage all of these years."

"You're not making any sense," Jo said. "Not that I should be surprised by that fact—I'm not prepared to believe a word you say."

"Josefina, my father was not responsible for your father's death. He was set up—you must believe that."

"What do you mean, he was set up?" Jo asked. "Who set him up?"

Diva shook her head. "I don't know all of the facts. What I do know is that Chico has made my father's life miserable ever since the murder of your father and the trial in Miami . . . but I don't know why."

"What does Chico have to do with all of

this?" Jo was starting to feel slightly dizzy. This whole situation was completely insane.

"Chico rules everything in Rio," Diva explained. "And he rules everything up above it, too, into America. Yes, he has provided for my family, and he made sure that my father was not wrongly sent to prison for the murder of your father . . . but he has had his own reasons for doing these things."

"None of this makes sense. I don't understand." Jo was trying not to feel sympathy for Diva, but it was difficult. The girl was a wreck.

"All Chico wanted was to keep his own hands from getting dirty," Diva said, her voice heavy with hate. "And he has kept my father in forced servitude for all of these years."

The full scope of what Diva was saying finally sank in. "Are you trying to tell me that *Chico* is the Big Boss?" Jo asked. "That's . . . well, it's impossible."

Diva snorted. "Believe me, it's more than possible. It's true." She paused. "And I believe that Chico is the man who murdered your father."

No. This conversation was now beyond totally insane. Diva was either out of her mind or the best liar Jo had ever had the displeasure to meet.

"But Chico's house is so modest . . . I mean, for a drug lord. Your *father's* house is the one that's huge and opulent."

Diva shook her head. "Josefina, you are very naive. That house where you and your friends are staying isn't where Chico really lives. He uses it as a cover so that he won't seem like such a wealthy man."

Jo's eyes widened. "And the mansion . . . ?"

"It is also his," Diva confirmed. "Not to mention two more houses—in other parts of Brazil—that he has bought in other people's names. As well as several homes in the United States. One in Miami."

"I don't believe you," Jo insisted, her head spinning. "Chico is so sweet. . . . He's like someone's grandfather." Like her *own* grandfather, in fact.

Diva laughed, but it was a laugh heavy with bitterness and frustration. "Aren't all evil men sweet on the surface, Josefina? Do you think they gain their power by showing their true selves to the world?"

Jo's head began to pound as she studied Diva's ravaged face. Once again, everything was spinning out of control. Jo had no idea who she could trust. Diva? Chico? The Tower agents? It was all a huge, ugly mess.

"Josefina, if you can find the gun that shot

the bullet that killed your father, then we can bring Chico to justice. It is our only hope."

"I'll think about what you've said," Jo told Diva after several long moments of tense, awkward silence. "That's all I can promise."

"Please, Josefina. Call me soon." With that parting remark, Diva disappeared into the dark Brazilian night.

Jo stood alone, feeling more isolated and confused than she had in her whole life. Only one thing was clear. This mission wasn't over. And it wouldn't *be* over—not until Jo learned the absolute truth about her father's death.

I t's official," Theresa said to Caylin the next afternoon. "This is the best tan I've ever had." Her careful use of the sunscreen had paid off. She had managed to get a tan without getting fried to a crisp in the process.

"That makes two of us," Caylin responded. "But Jo's still got us beat, even though she hasn't even sat down in the sun long enough to get a tan line. That's just so not like her."

"No kidding. If I didn't know better, I'd think that Jo was still deep into the mish."

Theresa glanced at Jo, who was sitting in a corner of the patio, shielded by a large umbrella. On the table in front of her was Theresa's laptop. Every time one of the girls walked over to check on Jo, she was engaged in a serene game of computer Monopoly.

Caylin took a sip from her tall, frosted glass of lemonade. "Well, she hasn't said anything about that gun since last night. That's a good sign . . . right?"

149

"I guess so. . . ." Theresa sighed. "It's just too bad that there isn't something we can do to help Jo get out of this black mood."

"Jo is one of the strongest people I've ever known. She'll bounce back when she's ready."

Theresa hoped Caylin was right. Jo had been forced to deal with a lot of heavy issues during this mission. But she was taking Diva's betrayal so personally . . . almost as if she couldn't bear to believe that yet one more person was willing to do evil in the world. Who was to say Jo would ever really get over the effects of this mission?

"We're not going to do any good by hovering over Jo and asking her how she feels every five seconds," Caylin continued. "The best thing we can do is have a good time ourselves—you know, teach by example."

Theresa laughed. "In that case, pass me that gold nail polish. I think I need a pedicure."

"Mind if I have a seat?" It was late afternoon by the time Jo had formulated a semifirm plan of action. And essential to that plan was a carefully orchestrated conversation with none other than Chico himself. She had found him in his den, smoking a pipe and relaxing with a café latte.

## Dial "V" for Vengeance

Chico glanced up from the Brazilian news paper he had been reading. "Of course, Jacinta. Please, have a seat."

The man was the picture of a clean conscience. In loose cotton pants, a traditional Brazilian shirt, and a pair of wire-rimmed reading glasses, Chico looked like any semiretired middle-class businessman. Jo sat down on the love seat opposite Chico's couch.

"I just wanted to thank you again for all your help," Jo began. "I mean, if it weren't for you, the man who killed my father would still be walking the streets."

Chico shrugged. "Was nothing, Jacinta. I am just happy that evil man is away now. It was good that I call The Tower with my information, yes?"

"Yes." Jo nodded. Okay. They were talking. . . . What now? "Do you have plans for the future, Chico?" she asked cautiously. "I mean, now that you don't have to worry about Diva and her father forcing you to do their dirty work?"

"I am an old man now. I will just sit in the sun and be lazy." He paused for a few moments, seemingly lost in the notion of permanent rest and relaxation. "Of course, there is part of me who wish I could have job like yours."

"Like mine?" Jo asked. Hmmm. Now they were getting somewhere. "What do you mean?"

"Tell me what it is like, working for the government in United States." His gaze was mild, but intent. "You must have exciting life, yes?"

Jo took a moment to gather her thoughts before she responded. She wanted to go at this part of their conversation with more than a little bit of imagination. "My job *is* pretty incredible. We get to do all kinds of James Bond stuff—you know, assassinations, bombings, the usual."

Chico raised his eyebrows. "That must be very difficult. I don't think I could do those things."

Jo shrugged. "If the ends justify the means, who cares what the price is?"

"I don't think I understand. What do you say—ends and means?" If Chico was faking the innocent routine, he was doing a darn good job of it.

"I'm just pointing out that sometimes it's necessary to kill someone. Not that I *want* to—we just have to." Lies, lies, lies. Diva wasn't the only person in Rio who could lie her tail off. Jo had gotten plenty of practice in the art of deception during her time as a Spy Girl.

"Oh, my, I could not do that. Never." Chico looked horrified by what Jo had said.

Jo put on a sad, almost tearful face. "Yes, it's

awful." She paused. "But there are other parts of the job that are a lot of fun."

"Oh yes?" Chico asked. "Tell me. I am just an old man. I don't know what is fun anymore."

Okay, they had established that Chico thought of himself as an old man. What a crime! "Well, we get to use lots of cool spy gadgets," Jo said, which was true enough. "Like, tiny cameras and microphones shaped like earrings and mini–computer modems . . . all that stuff."

"My, you girls *are* like James Bond." Chico still looked clueless.

"And I've gotten to play with lots of neato equipment," Jo continued. "We have access to all of this old knights' armor. . . ." Not. But whatever. "And one time I got to fire a Jack Major Longhorn pistol—this totally rare kind of gun."

There. A flicker. She had definitely seen a flash of interest in Chico's eye. An eye twitch wasn't a lot to go on, but at the moment, it had to be enough. . . .

Caylin stared at herself in the mirror. She had followed a Brazilian fashion mag's directions for the smoky-eyelid look, and the effect was nothing short of dazzling. Theresa, on the other hand, resembled a raccoon.

"Jo, you've got to come with us," Caylin said for the third time since dinner. "If you agree to go out, I'll even do your eyes so you look like an Egyptian princess."

"Thanks, guys, but I'm still feeling pretty drained." Jo was lounging on Caylin's bed, reading a random Harlequin romance that she had pulled from one of Chico's many bookcases. "I'm just going to hang out here and lose myself in the story of Adrianna and Storm."

"But Pedro is bringing two friends," Theresa pointed out. "Without you, Cay and I are going to be outnumbered."

"Yeah, it'll be La Americana all over again," Caylin added. "We'll be left to juggle the guys without you. And you know, that ain't right."

Jo shut the book. "Look. I'd love to, but I really think I'd just fall asleep at the table. My flirt switch is off tonight."

Caylin set down her mascara wand and turned to Jo. "Are you sure? 'Cause we can cancel with the hotties and stay here with you."

"Don't go nuts on me," Jo insisted. "There's, like, less than no point for you guys to miss out on possible action just because I want to stay in and eat bonbons all night." She paused. "Besides, I think I'm going to feel a whole lot better by tomorrow."

"Your wish is our command," Theresa said.

"But you'll be missing out—tonight I samba!"

Caylin laughed. She would have to remember to take some pictures of Theresa on the dance floor with her digital lash cam. If those photos wouldn't bring a smile to Jo's face, nothing would!

Storm had just ridden off on his white stallion, leaving Adrianna to take care of her family's farm all by herself. Ouch! Why were there always so many obstacles on the path to true love? Life just wasn't fair. Nor was it fair that Jo had to sit around and read this stupid book while she waited for Chico to hit the sack. She had been sitting in the den for almost two hours, waiting, waiting, waiting. . . .

"Jacinta, I leave now, yes?" Chico suddenly called from the doorway. Uh-oh. Was he going to the Big Boss mansion? That could spell major trouble. "Tonight I play cards at La Americana with my old friends."

It wasn't bed, but it would do. All she cared about was Chico staying as far away from her and Diva as possible. "Have a great time!" Jo said cheerily. "I'll see you tomorrow."

Chico frowned, his blue eyes concerned. "You will be good alone?"

Jo made a show of yawning and stretching her arms above her head. "Oh, don't worry about me. I'm just going to head up to bed and read for a while."

Chico nodded. "Have nice dreams, then, Jacinta."

Jo sat rigidly on the sofa as she waited for Chico's footsteps to fade down the hall. A moment later the front door opened and closed. Phew. He was gone. Time to set into motion part B of this totally insane plan. Jo picked up the phone at her side and dialed the number of El Centro.

"Yes?" Diva answered the phone on the first ring.

"It's on," Jo said quietly. "Meet me behind the house." Then she hung up the phone. Three, two, one, zero. Show time.

osefina? Is that you?" Diva's whispered voice was coming from somewhere behind a large patch of rosebushes.

"It's Jo, actually," she answered as Diva emerged from her hiding place. "Everyone calls me Jo—only my dad called me Josefina."

Diva smiled shakily. "Jo, then. Thanks for coming. I promise, I'm telling you the truth about Chico."

The girls walked toward the side of the house and crouched in the well of a door that led to the basement. "I don't know if you're telling the truth or not," Jo answered, not ready to risk being betrayed by her friend again. "But I'm here. So let's do this thing."

"We have to find the gun," Diva said. "The gun is the key."

Jo glanced around the backyard. "What's the security situation? Should we be expecting dogs, and alarms, and spotlights shining in our faces?" She hadn't noticed heavy-duty equipment during the last couple of days, but one never knew.

"Nope. Carlos is on duty tonight. He always drinks himself to sleep by eight o'clock or so."

Jo raised an eyebrow. "You don't say?"

Even in the dark, it was obvious that Diva was blushing. "What can I tell you? We went out for a while back when I was a rebellious young teenager."

Jo was tempted to laugh, but she didn't. "You're still pretty rebellious," she commented dryly. "Most good little girls would wind up arrested by government agents for participation in a major drug operation."

It was Diva's turn to glare. "Do you want to find the gun or not?"

"Any ideas on where it might be?" Jo asked. "This place is packed with stuff—a thorough search could take hours."

Diva nodded. "Chico showed me a secret door when I was a little girl. He was showing off for me . . . calling himself Uncle Chico and saying I was like his own daughter."

"What a scum." Slowly Jo was starting to buy Diva's story. There was too much detail, too much pain in her voice whenever she mentioned Chico or her father for Jo to believe that Diva was lying.

"The door leads to a private den," Diva

continued. "And at the back of the room there is another door—one that Chico warned me *never* to open."

"Do you think we'll find the gun in there?" Jo asked.

"Yes, that is what my heart tells me," Diva said. "If I'm wrong . . . well, then it could be anywhere."

"Do you remember how to open the secret door?" Jo asked.

"Yes—when I was young, we lived for a time in this house. I would sneak into that den often . . . but I never, ever had the *cojones* to go in that other room."

"No time like the present," Jo said. "You lead."

"This is it," Diva whispered ten minutes later. "This is the secret door."

The girls had slipped into the house through a first-floor window just in case Maria was still around and monitoring Jo's comings and goings. As Diva had predicted, Carlos was snoring loudly in the TV room off the front hall. Without a moment's hesitation, Diva had guided Jo down several long hallways. Finally she had stopped in front of a large oak book-case that Jo had noticed the day before. In fact, it had proved the home for *Storm Clouds through Town*.

159

"The door is disguised by a *bookcase?*" Jo whispered. "Man, this is like an episode of *Scooby Doo.* I just hope we have enough Scooby snacks to keep the dog quiet while we search for clues, Velma."

"What?" Diva stared blankly at Jo.

"Never mind. Just a bit of American pop culture humor." She pointed at the bookcase. "Open sesame." Jo was trying to keep the mood light, but her heart was racing a thousand beats a minute.

Diva removed a copy of Machiavelli's *The Prince*—how fitting—from the bookshelf. Then she reached to the back of the case and began to spin a combination lock. "I'll never forget this combination," she said. "Chico used to mouth the numbers as he opened the lock . . . and I've remembered them ever since."

"You really should be a spy," Jo commented. "Your instincts are amazing."

Jo heard a soft click from the back of the bookcase, and Diva smiled with satisfaction. "Stand back," she instructed.

As Jo stepped away from the bookcase, it began to move. After several seconds a door was revealed. "Wow!" Jo exclaimed softly. "This adventure is getting more Nancy Drewish by the second."

"Be serious, Jo," Diva warned. "You have no idea what Chico will do if he finds us. . . ."

Jo didn't need to be told twice that she was facing almost certain death if they were discovered by the wrong person. Whether or not that person was Chico . . . time would tell.

The girls slipped through the door and were immediately enveloped in one of the blackest blacks Jo had ever seen. She felt as if she were standing in a cave five miles below sea level. Yikes. Maybe she *should* have told Theresa and Caylin what she was up to. Until this moment she hadn't realized just how likely it was that she would never return from this leg of the mission. A girl could be locked up in this place a long time before anyone found her—especially if it turned out that Diva had lured her here on purpose out of sheer evil revenge. Now *that* would suck.

"Are you sure you're a good guy?" Jo whispered. "'Cause I'm putting a lot of trust in you right about now."

In the darkness Diva reached out and squeezed her hand. "Believe me, Jo, I'm in just as much danger as you are. It's only my love for my father that's allowing me to overcome my fears in order to prove his innocence."

"We'll do it for both of our dads, then," Jo said, echoing Diva's sentiments from the night before.

"Keep ahold of my hand and we'll go down the stairs together." Slowly the girls descended the steep stone staircase that led to the Big Boss's private sanctuary.

At the bottom of the stairs Diva stopped. "Aha!" She flipped a switch, and the room they had entered was immediately flooded with light.

"Nice clubhouse." The room was large, furnished with antiques and Tiffany lamps. A huge zebra skin rug covered much of the hardwood floor, and the heads of big-game animals lined the walls. Yep. This was pretty much what she'd expect the Big Boss's lair to look like. It was textbook.

Diva gazed around the room. "I used to come here and pretend that I was a princess locked away in a tower . . . waiting for my knight in shining armor. Back then, I didn't realize that I really was a prisoner."

"I guess that's the door with a capital *D*, huh?" Jo pointed to a normal-looking door at the back of the room.

Diva nodded. "Chico didn't even bother to put a lock on it. He knew that no one would ever dare go in there without permission."

"He didn't bet on us," Jo said. "Let's do it."

Her heart thumped painfully as the girls walked slowly toward the door. They had to find the gun. There were simply no ifs, ands, or buts about it. Jo didn't have a plan B. If she was ever going to discover the truth about her dad's murder, she was going to find it in that room.

"You do the honors, Jo," Diva said, gesturing toward the doorknob.

Jo grabbed the knob. It turned easily in her hand, and the girls tiptoed into no-man's-land. From the light in the den, Jo was able to spot a floor lamp next to the door. She turned on the light, then gasped.

"Holy mother . . . What is this place?" Diva whispered.

Jo was speechless. The room was nothing short of an arsenal. It was a weapons collector's heaven on earth. Swords, shields, and spears took up every inch of wall space. Several large gun cases dominated the small room. There was even an ancient suit of armor in the corner.

"I'm glad I never came in here," Diva whispered, her voice shaky. "I would have had nightmares for months—if I didn't accidentally shoot myself."

"The gun has to be here," Jo said. "I saw a picture of it in one of the articles I read online, so I'll know it when I see it."

"In that case, let's start the search," Diva

said. "I'm starting to feel a little claustrophobic—not to mention terrified."

Jo walked to one of the gun cases and peered inside. The thing was secured shut, but Jo predicted she could pick the lock with one of her Spy Girl gadgets in under fifteen seconds. She began to reach into her pocket but froze when she felt an unfamiliar presence behind her.

Jo whirled around. And there was Chico, looking not at all like the mild-mannered retiree who had bid her sweet dreams an hour ago.

"Looking for this, Josefina?" Chico asked. In his hand was the Jack Major Longhorn pistol that Jo had been searching for.

"Uh . . ." Plan B! Why didn't she have a plan B? Jo gulped. Had Diva set her up after all?

Before Jo had time to react to Chico's presence, Diva leaped out from behind the suit of armor and rushed their intruder. Diva dove toward Chico's back, but she was too late. He raised his arm and banged her on the head with the pearl-plated butt of the pistol.

Diva crumpled silently to the floor, knocked completely unconscious. Chico shook his head sadly. "Tsk, tsk. I always treated little Diva like she was my own daughter. It's such a shame when the young ones turn out to be ungrateful brats." He stared at Diva's lifeless body. "Still, if she wakes up, I may let her live. After all, she does such a magnificent job running El Centro for me."

Suddenly Chico's broken English had turned fluid. His whole persona had been a calculated, manipulative mask to protect himself from authorities. Dirtbag!

"You—you're evil," Jo said, staring into Chico's eyes. "How could anyone be so cruel?"

Diva had been telling the truth from the beginning. And Jo had doubted her. A wave of guilt washed over Jo as she remembered all the mean things she had said to her new friend during the last couple of days.

Chico was turning the gun over in his hand, studying the weapon from all angles. "You know, young Josefina, I found using this gun to take your father's life to be quite a pleasurable experience." He pulled a handful of bullets from his pants pocket and jingled them in the palm of his hand.

Jo felt a flush of blackness threaten to overtake her, but she fended it off. She wasn't going to give Chico the satisfaction of passing out. No, she was going to look into the eyes of her father's true murderer and tell him face-to-face how much she hated him.

"You are the lowest, most despicable form of

human life," Jo said, her voice like stone. "You didn't deserve to walk the same planet as my father."

As she spoke, Chico had been carefully loading the bullets into the pistol. Now he raised the gun. "Hush, Josefina. You teenagers are so rude."

Jo shut her mouth. With that gun in his hand, her options were limited at best.

"In fact, I enjoyed killing Judge Carreras so much that I have been unable to find a subject as worthy of these priceless bullets since." He took a moment to flash her a cold, brutal smile. "But you'll do quite nicely. A fine bit of symmetry, don't you think?"

He pointed the antique weapon directly at Jo's head. She shut her eyes. "I love you, Dad," she whispered.

"Prepare to join your beloved father, Josefina." He laughed. "You're going to die."

"Tell me what you want, what you really, really want!" Theresa shouted along to the music blaring in Club 222. "I say, if you wanna be—"

"Trixie, I never knew your real name was Off-key Spice," Caylin yelled in her ear as she danced past Theresa with Pedro.

Okay, so Theresa was never going to be Barbra Streisand. Wasn't she allowed to have a little fun once in a while? Even geeks had to let loose after a superhard, superemotional mission. And she *was* having a good time with . . . well, she had forgotten his name. But as long as the guy kept telling her how great she was at the samba, Theresa didn't care if his name was Satan.

Theresa leaned close to Pedro's friend. "Hey, what's your—" She broke off as she felt her minibeeper vibrating in the pocket of the ultra-tight black leather pants Caylin had persuaded her to wear. "Never mind."

She walked toward Caylin, struggling to get

the beeper out of her pocket. "We need to have a girl talk," she yelled in her fellow SG's ear. "Someone's calling."

Caylin danced away from Pedro, and the girls headed for a semiprivate, semi-well-lit corner of the club. "What's the message?" Caylin asked.

"I don't know. . . ." Theresa yanked on the beeper one more time, and it came free from the pocket. "But I'm never wearing these pants again." She glanced down at the pager. Uh-oh. It was a 911—from Danielle.

"Trouble," Theresa said to Caylin. They leaned over the small window on the top of the beeper and read the message:

> New Evidence Backup Deployed
> Arriving 2100 Hours
> Effect House Arrest Immediately

That was the sum total of the emergency message. The words were both cryptic and terrifying—the worst combination.

"What the—," Caylin started. "Ohmigod." She stared at Theresa. "Do you think this means . . . ?"

"Jo's theory," Theresa confirmed. "She was convinced that there was more to the mission than we thought."

"Which almost d-definitely means that D-Diva was telling the truth—," Caylin stuttered.

"And Chico is the Big Boss!"

The girls froze.

"Jo is home alone with him!" Caylin yelled. She glanced at her watch. "And 2100 hours is in . . . fifteen minutes."

"We've got to find her!" Theresa grabbed Caylin's arm, and the girls sprinted toward the exit. Jo's life was in serious jeopardy . . . and she probably didn't even know it.

*Click. Click. Click, click, click, click.* The gun hadn't gone off. Jo opened her eyes, realizing that she was still alive. Yes!

In front of her Chico was fumbling with the Longhorn. Oops. Apparently the pistol wasn't in the same prime condition it had been the morning the old man had used it to kill Judge Carreras. What a pity.

"Out of commission for too long, huh?" Jo asked. "Get used to it, Chico, old boy."

She reached behind her and pulled a five-foot spear from the wall. In one fluid motion Josefina Mercedes Carreras whipped the spear through the air low to the floor and swept Chico's legs out from underneath him. A deep sense of satisfaction settled over her as she watched him crash toward the cement floor.

169

"Ohhh!" Chico grunted as his head hit the ground.

*Bang!* The heretofore defunct Longhorn discharged one of its rare bullets—which landed in Chico's left thigh. His grip on the gun loosened, and it flew from his hand and landed several feet away from his body.

"Ooohhh . . . ," Chico moaned in pain, writhing on the cement floor. "I'm hurt! I'm hurt!"

"A fine bit of symmetry," Jo commented, taking delight in throwing Chico's words back in his ugly face.

She took a step toward the pistol and bent over to pick it up. But her hand froze. No. She couldn't pick up the filthy weapon that had taken her father's life.

Chico was staring at Jo's motionless hand. "Go ahead, Josefina. Pick up the gun. Point it right at my heart. Or blow my brains out if you prefer."

He was taunting her, daring Jo to sink to his own level. But she wasn't going to do it— she wouldn't give Chico the pleasure. "Forget it," Jo said. "I'm not scum like you. I'm not a killer."

Chico's face relaxed. She could read relief through the pain, and it infuriated her. "Aaahhh!" Jo screamed at the top of her lungs as she lifted the spear and held it over Chico's body.

"No!" Chico cringed in fear.

Jo let the spear drop to her side. "Psych." But Jo's heart wasn't really into her faked attack. This was no joke. She was looking for revenge—and justice.

"I can get the authorities here in a matter of minutes," Jo informed Chico. "This is it for you."

Chico was holding his leg, muttering to himself. "A girl. A man brought down by a useless girl. . . . Oh, the shame."

Jo glanced over at Diva, who had begun to moan. From this moment forward, she would think of her new friend as a sister. Truly, Jo owed her soul to the girl who had had the courage to pick up the phone and call The Tower. Maybe now there was something Jo could do to repay that favor.

"I will be the fool for all to see," Chico was blubbering. "Society will never again respect me. I will die in prison, a fool."

Jo leaned over Chico, still wielding the spear. "I'll make you a deal."

He stopped blathering long enough to look at her. "What is this deal?"

"If you vow that you and your associates will leave Diva and her family alone for the rest of their lives—that you'll never order revenge on them—I won't tell the authorities that I was the one who brought you down. I'll spare you the embarrassment."

Chico nodded. "Yes, on my honor, I vow. Just do not humiliate me before my people."

Jo stared at the pathetic old man in response. Let the Big Boss worry about his manhood for a few moments, she figured. Jo liked to see him squirm.

"Over here!" Caylin screamed. She and Theresa had just located the secret door.

Danielle raced to their side. "Here, people!" she cried.

Flashlights in hand, Caylin, Theresa, Danielle, and about twenty other American and Brazilian agents thundered down the stone stairway. At the bottom they rushed through Chico's private den and burst through yet another door.

"Jo!" Theresa yelled. "Jo!"

Caylin stopped short behind Theresa. Thank goodness. Jo was sitting on top of an antique desk, staring at a writhing Chico as if she were in shock—but by all appearance physically unharmed. On the floor Diva was lying down, her eyelids fluttering.

"Are you all right?" Caylin had run to Jo's side.

"I'm fine now. But I think Diva is going to have a headache in the morning."

Tower agents flooded the small room, surrounding Chico. There must have been a dozen semiautomatic guns pointed at the monster's head. "I was shot!" Chico yelled. "Some men ran in here and shot me before those brats came in!"

Caylin glanced at Jo. "Is that what happened?"

Jo shrugged. "Close enough."

"Oh, Jo, we should have listened to you," Theresa said, approaching Jo and wrapping her in an embrace. "You were right about Diva all along!"

"Let's go, Chico," Danielle said. "We'll worry about the mystery men who shot you back at Tower headquarters." She turned to the Spy Girls. "By the way, I spoke to Uncle Sam on the way over here, and he assured me that you're all getting a raise."

Several agents hoisted Chico to his feet and more or less dragged him toward the door. "I don't know who they were. . . . They were wearing masks."

"You'll have plenty of time to think about the shooters' identities while you're rotting in jail," one of The Tower agents assured him.

Caylin knelt beside Diva as Chico's hysterical

voice faded in the distance. "Diva? Are you okay?"

Danielle gently felt Diva's head, looking for signs of injury. "I think she's going to be fine. But Jo is right—that'll be a nasty bump in the morning."

Caylin turned her attention back to Jo. "Are you really okay? Chico didn't hurt you?"

Jo smiled. It was a small, slightly sad smile, but a smile nonetheless. "I really think I am going to be okay now . . . better than okay."

Caylin grinned. At last, their friend had the answers she had been searching for. Now Jo could begin the healing process in earnest.

"*Papá!*" Diva suddenly screamed.

Caylin whirled around. The man they had mistakenly believed was the Big Boss was standing at the door of the arsenal, grinning at his daughter. Diva sprang off the floor and launched herself into her father's arms.

"I am free," he told Diva, holding her close. "At last, our whole family is free."

Caylin felt tears well in her eyes and turned to look at Jo. There was a smile on Jo's face and tears in her eyes as she stared at Diva's reunion with her father. Finally—they had found a happy ending.

\*     \*     \*

## Dial "V" for Vengeance

An hour later Theresa studied the faces of the people who had gathered in the conference room of The Tower's Rio headquarters. For the first time in days, she felt totally relaxed. Diva was sitting in between her father and Jo, alternately laughing and crying as the group pieced together the whole story of what had gone down—both during the mission and four years ago, the day Jo's father had been murdered.

"Chico wanted me to kill your father," Mr. Sanchez—yes, she had finally learned Diva's last name—was saying to Jo. "He told me that if I didn't do the job, he would make life very hard for me and my family."

"What happened?" Caylin asked.

"I saw Jo and her father, talking so happily with each other. I had a daughter—Diva—who was the same age as Josefina." He paused to give Diva a brief hug. "Well, as soon as I saw them, I knew there was no way I could go through with it. I could not kill a man."

"Go on," Theresa urged him.

"Chico was waiting in the getaway car. He sensed my hesitancy, and he followed me to the car where Jo and her father were sitting. Finally he came up behind me and shot Judge Carreras with that pistol."

"I knew I had seen your face," Jo said quietly. "But at the time I didn't realize that it was

Chico who put the gun to my father's head. . . . Everything happened so fast that day." Tears were streaming down her face.

"Anyway, as soon as he pulled the trigger, Chico ran away and jumped into the getaway car. I was left there to be arrested at the scene of the crime."

Caylin continued to listen to Mr. Sanchez's story. It was a prime example of the truth being stranger than fiction. After Mr. Sanchez's arrest, Chico had hired a high-powered attorney. Between the lawyer, Chico's contacts in the Miami police department, and the truly insufficient evidence, Mr. Sanchez was eventually acquitted. After that, Chico had followed up on his promise to make Mr. Sanchez's life miserable. Since he had the real murder weapon, he swore that if Diva's father ever disobeyed him again, Chico would get in touch with American authorities and anonymously supply the missing pistol.

"But I have always been haunted by that day," Mr. Sanchez said. He turned to Jo. "I don't know if you can ever forgive me for being there that morning, Josefina, but I want you to know that I will live with the events of that morning for the rest of your life."

Jo turned to Diva's father. "I forgive you," she said. "And I think my father would have forgiven you, too. Your family was as much a victim in all of this as mine."

"I'm just glad that Mr. Sanchez had enough hard evidence to identify Chico as the real Big Boss," Theresa commented. "If The Tower hadn't realized how much danger Jo was in from Mr. Sanchez's statements in jail, who knew what might have happened to our third Spy Girl?"

Jo smiled. "Don't forget those mystery men. They were there."

Danielle frowned. "I'm not even going to go there. . . ."

"Let's focus on the fact that Chico's reign of terror is finally over," Jo said. "I think we all have a reason to celebrate."

Diva leaned over and hugged Jo. "You are all our family now," she said, tears running down her face. "We are forever in your debt."

Caylin hadn't realized that her own cheeks were wet with tears. All of their missions had been amazing. But this one—it had been the best. Their week in Brazil was one the Spy Girls would remember forever.

"I feel truly peaceful for the first time in four years," Jo said quietly. "And I think my dad would be proud of me."

"I'm sure he *is* proud, Jo," Caylin assured her. "He's probably watching us right now and smiling."

After the post-post-sting debriefing, the girls

had retired to a hotel close to the airport. They had changed into their pajamas, but all three of them were still wide awake. Especially Jo. She had come through this rite of passage intact, and she felt better for having faced the past. For the first time in four years, she felt that she could remember her father without dwelling on the tragedy of his death. And that was a gift for which she would always be grateful.

"I think we all learned a lot on this mission," Theresa commented. "For instance, in the future, if Jo tells me I can trust someone, I'll listen to her." She grinned sheepishly. "I can't believe I ever doubted Diva's sincerity."

"We all did," Caylin reminded her. "Let's face it. The evidence didn't exactly work in her favor."

Jo was about to chime in encouraging words to Theresa when there was a knock on the door of the hotel room. "Let me guess. It's the Avon lady."

She went to the door, half expecting to find one of Chico's emissaries waiting with a gun in his hand. Instead she opened the door and found an ultracute Tower agent.

"I have a little present for you girls," he told them. "Courtesy of Uncle Sam." He handed Jo a white envelope, then took off down the hall.

# Dial "V" for Vengeance

"What's in it?" Theresa asked, climbing off the bed. "Are we getting a bonus on top of our raise?"

Jo opened the envelope and pulled out three tickets. "They're VIP passes to the big Kinh-Sanh benefit concert that's going to be at Madison Square Garden next week," she announced.

Caylin bounced excitedly. "New York, New York! Hey, you think this is another vacation?"

"Maybe." Jo studied the tickets, a smile on her face. "Or maybe . . . we're about to start a new mission?"

"Fasten your seat belts, Spy Girls," Theresa said. "I think we're in for another thrill ride."

*About the Author*

Elizabeth Cage is a saucy pseudonym for a noted young adult writer. Her true identity and current whereabouts are classified.

Printed in the United States
By Bookmasters